TEN NASTY LITTLE TOADS

D0305174

First published in 2018 by Zephyr, an imprint of Head of Zeus
This paperback edition published in 2019 by Zephyr

Text copyright © Steve Cole, 2018
Illustrations copyright © Tim Archbold, 2018

The moral right of Steve Cole to be identified as the author of this work and
Tim Archbold to be identified as the illustrator of this work has been asserted
in accordance with the Copyright, Designs and Patents Act of 1988.

All rights reserved. No part of this publication may be reproduced, stored in
a retrieval system, or transmitted in any form or by any means, electronic,
mechanical, photocopying, recording, or otherwise, without the prior
permission of both the copyright owner and the above publisher of this book.

This is a work of fiction. All characters, organizations, and events
portrayed in this novel are either products of the author's
imagination or are used fictitiously.

9 7 5 3 1 2 4 6 8

A catalogue record for this book is available from the British Library.

ISBN (PB): 9781786699329
ISBN (E): 9781786699305

Printed and bound in Serbia by Publikum
Designed by Sue Michniewicz

Head of Zeus Ltd
First Floor East
5–8 Hardwick Street
London EC1R 4RG

WWW.HEADOFZEUS.COM

TEN NASTY LITTLE TOADS

STEVE COLE

Illustrated by
TIM ARCHBOLD

ZEPHYR

GREETINGS!

Big, fat, warty welcome wishes from me,
Madame Rana!
Why have you picked up this book?
I can think of four possible reasons.

1. You are
a nasty little toad and
want to look up your
friends.

2. You want to read
some mind-boggling, brain-
blowing, totally twisted toady
tales that will make you laugh,
gasp, groan, gulp and fall out of
bed. (Even if you are not reading
them in a bed – SPOOKY!)

3. You were reaching for some other book but MYSTERIOUSLY picked up this one instead, because you are no match for my wondrously witchy powers!

4. You sensed that there are in fact TWELVE horrid little toads in this book, rather than the ten that were promised on the front cover, and wanted to check for yourself. Well, clever-socks, the two extra toads are SIBLINGS, and so – according to the latest copy of *Ye Olde Witch Booke of Toady Thinges* by Mrs Slugsnail Toadiface, published in 1422 – siblings always count as half a toad each. Don't blame me, blame her – silly old bat. However, if it helps to think of this book as *Ten Nasty Little Toads and Two Odd Frogs*, then I won't stop you – fair enough?

Anyway! Whatever your reason for being here, WELCOME! I hope you will enjoy the contents of this book. But, please, DO NOT attempt to imitate any of the toadish behaviour you will encounter. THERE COULD BE CONSEQUENCES . . .

Toodle-toadle-loo!

Madame R

Dirty Little Toad!

 I've heard you on bath night. Yes, yes, I have. I've heard you moan and mumble and groan and grumble as you drag yourself upstairs. 'WHY do I have to have a bath AGAIN?'

You even complain about having to wash your face in the morning. I know, I've heard you then too. Those few extra seconds spent fooling with a flannel – how you begrudge them. And how many times have you always accidentally 'forgotten' to clean behind your ears, mmmm?

I know how it is. You're a busy person with things to do, and boring grown-ups keep burbling on about how you must brush your teeth at least twice a day (even though your baby teeth are meant to fall out anyway!) and you must wash your hands after going to the toilet (YAWN!) and after handling your pet (it's not like Flopsy is even dirty!). Oh – and before meals (even though you'll be using a knife and fork and your fingers won't even TOUCH the food!) and make sure the water is warm, thank you very much, not freezing cold (like it makes a difference!) All that soapy, hot watery DO-THIS and DO-THAT.

Doesn't it seem *endless*?

Well, that nagging might make you cross, but that's because you haven't met a child of your age who *doesn't* wash her hands or face or behind her ears – or anywhere at all, for that matter. You haven't met a girl who hasn't had a bath or a shower in YEARS.

But you're going to meet her now. And a proper little toad she is too.

May I introduce to you Cherry Oddfellow: part-girl, part-mudslide? She has not washed for three years, two months and twenty-seven days.

'How can this be?' you may ask. 'How did she get away with that?'

She got away with it through a mixture of stealth and extreme tantrums.

Her mum and dad worked very hard and came home terribly tired each evening. They wanted nothing more than a quiet night – and if it was bath night, then all they got was a screaming nightmare.

Cherry simply *hated* being clean, right from the start.

As a small child, she would cling to the towel rail to avoid her bath, shrieking the house down.

When her parents tried to give her showers instead, she would swing like Spider-Man from the showerhead and pull it off the wall.

Even a trip to the swimming baths would end in disaster, as Cherry knew there was one sure way to escape a dip. I'm sure you know EXACTLY what I'm talking about.

What a revolting little toad she was!

The older she got, the worse the problem became.

'Wash your face for school, Cherry,' her mum would say.

Cherry would immediately charge about like a ferret on fire, wrestling with every sink in the house before she was worn out enough for Mum to grab her with a sponge.

'Did you wash your hands for supper?' Cherry's dad would ask.

Cherry would immediately thump him with the nearest blunt instrument and throw heavy objects through the

bathroom window before her mum got lucky with the hand
sanitizer.

'It's just a phase she's going through,' Mr Oddfellow
reckoned fondly, rubbing his jaw.

The final straw that broke the (very mucky) camel's back arrived, as I mentioned earlier, three years, two months and twenty-eight days ago: 'Cherry,' said Mrs Oddfellow one Friday afternoon, 'we thought we might take a little holiday. A city break.'

'Where?' Cherry demanded.

'Why, in the delightful county of Somerset,' Mr Oddfellow said brightly.

'Somerset?' Cherry's mud-brown eyes narrowed in suspicion. 'Whereabouts in Somerset?'

'Er, well . . .' Mr Oddfellow gulped. 'We were thinking about the fine city of Bath.'

'BAAAAATH?' With a wailing war cry, Cherry ran outside and started biting the car tyres to cause multiple punctures. Her dad had to jet-wash her with the patio cleaner to make her stop. (Little did he know that *this* was to be the last dip in water she would have for years!)

Screaming and spluttering, Cherry fled inside the house, swallowed the car keys and barricaded herself in her bedroom so no one could take her anywhere.

This was the regrettable day Mr and Mrs Oddfellow had to face facts – they simply did not possess the patience, strength and stamina required to keep their growing daughter in the same room as a loofah long enough for any real cleaning to occur.

And so, they took that dread decision to wash their hands of washing their daughter. They wrote a note to school explaining that Cherry was allergic to being clean: could she please be excused showers after PE? They also supplied the name of a firm that made cheap clothes pegs and advised all teachers to keep a window open in the classroom for the safety of Cherry's fellow pupils.

'It won't be for long,' said Mrs Oddfellow. 'It's just that silly, longer-than-expected phase she's still going through.'

Mr Oddfellow nodded. 'When she *really* starts to pong, she'll start bathing again. Just you wait.'

Well, the Oddfellows *did* wait.

But did Cherry change her mind? She did not.

Refusing to wash or bathe or even rinse her hands, she gradually became more and more engrimed with mud and dirt. Her parents learned to ignore it, and stuffed earplugs up their noses to stop the stink.

The closest Cherry ever came to a shower was when she was caught in the rain; then you could see the mud trickling down her face from her filthy red hair.

Did I say red? *Once* it was that beautiful colour. But

since she never washed it or brushed it, it became a thick thatch of dirt, dust and straw. Weeds began to grow in it. A crow mistook it for an empty nest and moved right in. Cherry didn't shoo it away – she was glad of the company, since her friends no longer went near for fear of passing out from the pong.

Her parents were appalled. 'A crow!' cried Mrs Oddfellow. 'In her hair!'

Mr Oddfellow sank a little further into his newspaper. 'I'm sure they're all the rage with young people these days.'

The crow, naturally, preferred the outdoors life, so Cherry took to staying in the garden whatever the weather. Her shoes got very muddy. One day she found a worm living in her sock. (It would've preferred her shoe, but it didn't want to be spotted by the crow.)

'Ahhhh!' she sighed as it curled around her muddy toes. 'Lovely and squishy!'

Keen not to disturb her new friends –
especially after the crow had laid some eggs
in her hair – Cherry decided it was high time
she stopped changing her clothes. She wore the same
things, day after day, week after week, month after
month, and, of course, they became dirtier and
dirtier. Her mum and dad begged her to change her
mind (and her underwear) but she refused.

Finally, Mrs Oddfellow lost the last shreds of
her patience. 'This nonsense has gone far enough,
young lady,' she cried. 'If you don't get changed out of those
revolting garments and have a jolly good bath RIGHT NOW,
I'm going to—'

But the threat set to emerge from her throat died on her
lips, for Cherry had not wasted her time outside. She had
spent much of it training her crow to a very high standard.
Now, on her command, the belligerent bird burst from
Cherry's dirty thatch and pecked Mrs Oddfellow on the
head. With a shriek of dismay, the unfortunate woman fled
trembling into the arms of her husband. Sadly, they weren't
very comforting arms because Mr Oddfellow had fainted
and fallen to the floor, suffering as he did from an irrational
fear of crows.

Cherry chuckled. Now she knew she had total control
over her parents – and how she *crowed* about it! *When the
chicks are old enough to fly, I'll make them peck Mum and*

Dad too, she thought. *And then I'll train the worm to be an attack worm. Ha, ha, ha!* (In the event, this particular training was stopped by the baby chicks who, while admiring the fighting spirit of the worm, admired his taste rather more.)

As time went by, Cherry barely noticed the weeds growing out of her hair, or the moss that clung to her grotty clothes, or the grass sprouting from her filthy hands and legs. She thought she looked quite fabulous!

'I'm the Green Queen!' she declared proudly in the playground, while everyone ran from her powerful pong. 'The First Lady of Filth! The Empress of Muddiness!' She lay down in the sun on the playing fields and sighed happily. The bell went for afternoon school, but Cherry didn't bother getting up . . . she supposed her boring old teachers would call her after a while.

But they didn't.

With a thrill, Cherry realised that here, lying on the grass of the playing fields, she blended right in. No one could spot her!

Of course, the fact that she was so stinky and unpleasant that no one *wanted* to spot her didn't occur to Cherry. She just

lay there and congratulated herself on her brilliant mucky disguise. She stayed there for the rest of the day, happily snoozing.

Mr Oddfellow asked: 'How was school today?'

'School was GREAT,' Cherry said. 'I was very happy to be there.'

Her father was pleased. He didn't realise that school had been 'great' for Cherry because she had been lounging about in the field.

Because she'd got away with one day off, Cherry decided to try for another.

It worked.

The teachers were actually quite relieved that Cherry wasn't there; the Head had been about to insist that gas masks be worn in Cherry's class at all times, and no one was eager for that. So when she didn't show up, they didn't ask why, they just thanked their lucky stars. You can't blame them; with her revolting habits, Cherry had turned everyone against her. She spent the whole of the next day invisible to the naked eye, looking like nothing more than a lump of mud and turf that had learned how to breathe.

By now, the crow and her family had flown away. Even they couldn't bear the smell of Cherry Oddfellow a moment longer. Still, the bugs that squirmed and wriggled between her clothes and her skin didn't mind the stink, and Cherry

didn't mind them either. She was quite happy, lying on the school fields in the sunshine doing nothing. While her classmates worked like good, well-behaved children, Cherry simply drifted off to sleep. The grass was quite long, and ever so comfortable.

What Cherry didn't know, as she slept, was that the playing fields were about to be mowed.

She didn't hear the sound of the groundskeeper starting up the big ride-on lawnmower.

She didn't hear the throaty growl of the engine, or the buzz of the mower blades as they spun hungrily into life.

(Dear reader, do *promise* me you will NEVER get in the way of a lawnmower!)

Didn't hear the **MWAAAAAAAAAAW** of the mower as it slowly rumbled towards her, slicing through the grass, getting closer . . .

(Promise me!)

Closer . . .

(Cross your heart and hope never to be mown!)

Closer and closer *still* came the mower . . .

And then it went past her, missing her by a matter of centimetres. *Phew!*

Unfortunately, the groundskeeper noticed he'd missed a bit and so put the mower into reverse.

Bu**ZZZZZZZZZZZ**! The lethal lawnmower blades chopped through Cherry's hair, leaving her with a very

strange haircut. Rudely awakened, she leaped up in terror and shrieked at the top of her lungs. The poor groundskeeper got such a shock he fell off his mower – which promptly went out of control.

'*EEEEEEEEEEEEEEEK!* Cherry was chased by the runaway mower twice around the school field and then into the shower block.

Luckily, a quick-thinking PE teacher saw what was happening and acted swiftly and bravely.

He didn't turn off the mower. He turned on the SHOWERS.

WHooooooooSH! Powerful blasts of hot water hit Cherry from ten different nozzles. Exhausted from her run, she was too weak to crawl away. Water and steam engulfed her. Mud

poured from her like lava from a volcano. Moss and grass
that had stuck to her skin for years began to fall free . . .

In fact, the drains and gutters were soon so thick with dirt
that they became blocked. The water level began to rise

Meanwhile, the runaway mower had crashed into the
wall of the shower block, its engine overheating. **FWOMPH!**
Flames burst from the unfortunate machine.

'Call the fire brigade!' wailed the groundskeeper.

Cherry, meanwhile, had managed to turn off the
showers. She was still disgustingly dirty – years of muck
won't wash away just like that – and what filth she had left
she was determined to keep. Dripping mud and slime, she
stomped from the shower block and pulled open the outside
door . . .

Only to find she was directly in the path of a firefighter's hose!

SWoooooooSH!

The almighty blast soaked Cherry from head to foot like a freezing, high-powered waterfall. It swept her back into the hot-water-filled changing rooms and swilled her about like old toilet paper being flushed down the pan.

Realising her mistake, and with the mower's flames safely extinguished, the firefighter turned off her hose. The groundskeeper clapped politely.

And the PE teacher peered through the steam and saw an odd sight come splashing uncertainly into view, wrapped in a wet towel.

It was Cherry Oddfellow.

She looked . . .

Clean.

She even *smelled* clean.

'Cherry!' cheered the PE teacher. 'Finally, you've cleaned up your act!'

Cherry wasn't listening. She was too busy rolling in the nearest flowerbed, determined to get dirty again as quickly as possible.

But, since then, staying filthy's not been quite so easy for her.

Because now, her parents know just what to do.

The Fire Chief has given them special permission to call up twice a week on Cherry's bath nights. Firefighters are very public-spirited, and can always use a bit of target practice for their hoses.

However fast Cherry runs, they always hose her down in . . .

The End

Disgusting Little Toad!

Jacques LaConk. Now *there* was a slimy little stinker.

Oh, he was nice enough on the surface. He had been raised very well by an elderly aunty: he said please and thank you, he spoke when he was spoken to and stayed quiet when he wasn't.

'Such a nice young man,' people said of him.

But those people didn't know what he was up to when they weren't looking. And since his aunty was too frail to climb the stairs, once he was in his bedroom or the bathroom, he had no fear of being disturbed.

You see, unpleasant though it is for me to say, I'm afraid Jacques was one of those boys who was fascinated by . . . stuff.

Bodily stuff.

You know – the stuff that runs and dribbles. The stuff you have to squeeze or pick.

I don't suppose you enjoy having a cold. Well, *Jacques* does. Each sneeze and cough is a journey of discovery for him! He never uses a tissue either, preferring to catch what comes out in the palm of his hand.

Of course, not everything unpleasant comes out through the face. When most of us need to break wind – or fart, if you prefer – we do so, and swiftly move on with our lives.

For Jacques, however, this *was* his life. He paid the keenest attention to the tiniest bottom-burp and would have an empty jam jar ready to bottle that natural gas. **FRRRRRP!** Once it was trapped, he'd wait a while, and then take off the lid and inhale the thick, cabbagey scent. That done, he'd write a brief review of the fart in the notebook he always kept handy – for instance: *WOW! THAT SMELLS LIKE A DEAD DONKEY IN A FIELD OF ROTTEN EGGS! 9.5/10 –* and he kept his favourite farts in jars on a shelf in his bedroom.

What a *disgusting* little toad!

You might wonder why Jacques was like this.

Well, he lived with his aged aunty, whose legs were extremely wobbly. She home-educated him, and that left her so weary she couldn't do very much besides sit down, sleep

26

and watch old movies on the television. She hadn't ventured upstairs in the house since 1986, decades before Jacques was born. So, when Jacques was let loose up there he found it full of disgusting discoveries. The carpets had become deserts of dust. The remains of dead mice and rats littered the landing, as did their desiccated droppings. Damp floorboards lay slowly rotting. Slimy mould and fungus grew on the walls . . .

This was the home that shaped him. So, really, Jacques' fascination with his own yucky stuff cannot come as too much of a surprise.

It used to take Jacques' aunty all day just to go to the corner shop and back – longer if there was a wind blowing. So Jacques had a lot of time on his hands: time enough to keep track of all the nasty, sticky bits that his body could produce. And GOODNESS me, his body could produce SUCH an incredible amount!

If he saw someone pick their nose he'd laugh in their face. 'Call that a bogey?' he'd sneer. 'Now, THIS is a bogey!' And he'd hook one out as big as a stoat's head.

Such mighty mucus sounds like the stuff of fables, and yet for Jacques, it was merely average. He had been blessed with a truly remarkable nose. It wasn't unduly big, or particularly red . . . but it was *outstandingly* snotty. Like the magic porridge pot in the old story, his nose could never be emptied. And Jacques liked nothing more than to extend the index finger of his right and left hands at once and explore the interior of his nostrils like an archaeologist questing for rare specimens.

Now, I know that YOU have picked your nose from time to time. Yes, you have, admit it. That doesn't make you too much of a toad; most children enjoy a good haul from the hooter. However, toadier types will wipe

Party piece

their finger-findings on the wall, or the carpet, or – so much nastier – pop the bogeys in their mouth. This is REVOLTING, yes ... but at least it is good for your immune system, and leaves no trace.

Jacques LaConk, however, looked

Glob grabber down his nose at ordinary nose-pickers. He was in another class altogether. Jacques would dedicate HOURS to rummaging in his nostrils, sometimes whole DAYS.

For many years, as a younger boy, Jacques had noshed his own nose-nuggets by the kilogram; in the end he'd had to give up because he was getting too full and missing out on Aunty's sweets and cake. So, he'd simply flick his nose-nastiness under the bed ... along with many other lumps of unloveliness.

Average ear wax extractor

Super scratcher.

It was a shame, because Jacques had built himself a rather fine high-rise bed: the only modern thing in the house. He'd tried sleeping in a regular bed, but the floorboards were mouldy,

Slimy specimen

Ordinary nose wiper

and the mould ate into the bedposts and made them rot. Three of his beds had collapsed in as many years! The high-rise bed was built on a frame made of strong plastic and he reached the mattress by climbing a short ladder. A black curtain drawn

across the frame hid the space beneath the bed – a space that in normal bedrooms would be taken up with games or cuddly toys.

But in Jacques' room, that space was damp and slimy, of course.

Nit nest

Sneaky swipe

So whenever he had a good poke about in his ear, his armpits or his belly button to see what wax, fluff or yucky stuff he might find – and once he'd recorded his findings – **Flick!** – through the black curtain and under the bed it went. It was his hope that the goop would cover the mouldy floorboards with a strong, sticky layer to seal in the slime.

'Rummage, Pick! Consider, Flick!
Under the bed; Nothing more said.'

Every now and then, drifting off to sleep with a thumb up his nostril, he wondered . . . He'd flicked so much stuff through those curtains over the years, but had never once peeked to see what it looked like. His aunty had never peeked either, since her legs were too wobbly to drag herself up the stairs; even so, Jacques suspected she would not approve of his wasting so much storage space.

What did it look like by now, all that gunk under the bed?

Then, one fateful night, Jacques had a bad dream. In that bad dream, he was lying in bed.

'Jacques . . .' came a deep, warbling, gurgling voice from under the bed. 'Jacques . . . I am hungry. Feed me! Make me BIG! Make me FAT!'

Dream-Jacques jumped into action, picking his nose and flicking it into the darkness under the bed, over and over, first the left nostril, then the right, his fingers a blur as they scraped about. **Flick – SPLAT! Flick – SPLAT!** Over and over and over and over . . .

The monster sighed and moaned. 'TOO SLOW!' it rasped. 'I THINK I'LL COME OUT AND HELP MYSELF.'

'No!' cried Dream-Jacques, clutching his conk in terror. 'Please . . .'

He heard sticky, dragging footsteps . . . then the dark curtains opened and a huge, hideous beast loomed over him, goo dripping from its lumpy limbs like mozzarella from a pizza as its huge fingers reached for Jacques' nose —

'NOOOO!' Jacques woke and sat bolt upright in bed, panting for breath. He tried to control his breathing and calm his racing heart.

He froze. Was that a noise?

Yes. Yes, it was.

A creaking, groaning sort of a noise sounded from the space beneath the bed, behind the curtain. It was as if something had shifted.

But what?

Jacques shrank under his bed sheets in terror. What if he hadn't been dreaming? What if there REALLY *was* a beast down there?

'Y-y-y-you want feeding?' he whispered. 'Here!' Frantically he flicked his crusty catches through the curtain. Over and over and over and over . . . until finally, he fell asleep.

When Jacques woke in the morning, he felt horribly tired. That actually worked out pretty well as he found he had a lot of gritty, yellow-brown sleep in his eyes,

which he quickly flicked under the bed too. He was still
worried by his dream – and whether it was only a dream.

I know, he thought, *I'll drag Aunty up here and she
can look*. But Jacques knew that she was frail and weak, and
the sight of his beast might well finish her off.

Well, then, I'll bring a friend to look. But of course, he
had no friends, unless you counted his jars of captured wind.
(And if you *did* count them, you'd find he had four hundred
and seven of them.)

I'm being silly, he decided at last, and got on with
the serious business of picking, sniffing, examining and
recording.

Only at bedtime, in his dark room, did the fear return.

And so did the quiet, creaking groan.

'It's real! It's true!' Jacques whimpered. 'A hungry beast is coming to get me because I can't feed him fast enough!' And as the midnight hours passed, Jacques' feverish fingers gathered a scandalous amount of fluff from between his sweaty toes and enough earwax to make an ornamental candle. He flicked the lot through the gap in the curtain until eventually, exhausted, he fell asleep.

Next night, exactly the same thing happened. And the night after that too: the same groan from under the bed, the same high-pitched 'EEK!' from Jacques, the same frantic burrowing for body-gunk and the same *flick-flick-flick* of his under-the-bed delivery.

The pattern repeated itself each night for over a fortnight. But the groaning sound did not go away.

It got louder. Longer. A protesting, rumbling groan. Sometimes Jacques even heard it during the day. 'I can't be imagining that,' he murmured.

It sounded like something was shifting from side to side, growing stronger, straining to be free.

That night, in desperation, Jacques began to open his fart jars and throw them under the bed, in the hope they would either feed the beast or gas it to death. There was no comforting squelch of glass on damp floorboards. There was only a **THUNK!** and a rapid rocking to and fro, as if something were laughing . . .

This hectic nightly activity was taking its toll on Jacques. He was growing paler and thinner. He felt sleepy all the time, and gave up recording everything that came out of him. Worse still, his nose seemed to be drying up like a spent coal mine, and it was growing harder and harder to find rich seams.

GROAANNNNNN came the noise from under the bed.

'I'm doing my best!' Jacques hissed. 'You ungrateful monster!'

GROOOOAAAAAAANNNNNNNNNNN came the protesting reply.

'I'm flicking you as much goop as I can!'

GROOOAAAAAAAAAAAANNNNNNNNNNNNNNN.

Finally, Jacques had his finger wedged so far up his nostril it nearly poked his eye out from the inside. 'Ouch!' He jumped in pain and banged his head against the wall. 'Ouch! Ouch! Ouch!'

'Whatever are you doing, dear?' called his aunty from downstairs.

'Nothing,' Jacques wailed. But the pain had made him angry, and anger had given him sudden courage. 'I can't go on like this,' he said. 'My nose will fall off before long. This stupid beast will just have to understand, *I can't give him any more!*'

Before he could dither and change his mind, Jacques switched on the lamp, climbed down from his cabin bed, grasped the curtains in both hands . . .

And . . .

Eyes closed . . .

Breath held . . .

Sweat dripping . . .

Heart thumping . . .

Knees knocking . . .

Jacques swept the curtains open.

He gasped.

There was no beast under his bed.

But there was *something* there: a monster-sized, greasy, grotty ball of old snot, wax, foot-pickings, hair and fluff, chewed fingernails, jars of fart and worse. It had grown as big as an armchair, and rocked gently from side to side.

Fascinated, Jacques squeezed in beside the enormous statue of grot that he had accidentally created. To his toadish eyes, it was BEAUTIFUL. He nuzzled up to it and hugged it close.

It was only then that
he realised just what had
been making the quiet,
groaning, protesting
noise for all those weeks.

The noise was
coming from the soggy
floorboards. They had
been straining under the
sheer weight of Jacques'
giant gobbet of horror.
Now Jacques had added
his own weight too, the
floorboards couldn't take any more – and finally gave up
with a splintering KK-KRAKKKKKKK!

Jacques screamed as he
fell through his bedroom floor,
crashed through the ceiling of
his aunty's room and landed
with a SPLAT.

The good news was
that the grot-ball broke
Jacques' fall, so that he
only broke both arms
instead of his neck.

The bad news

was that it exploded on impact into a billion bits. His aunty screamed as her room was pebble-dashed with the awful ingredients – a scream that stopped suddenly when a ghastly lump socked her in the mush and she fell over backwards.

The better news was that it took poor Aunty just two-and-a-half hours on her wobbly legs to reach the telephone and call for an ambulance.

And the best news of all was that Jacques' two broken arms in plaster made picking his nose, catching his sneezes, digging out earwax and wiping his bottom quite impossible for several weeks.

Unfortunately, he practised day and night with his toes so he could continue his revolting work . . . and, of course, he succeeded in . . .

The End

TOAD JOKES

Why are frogs the worst drivers?
The cars are always being
toad away!

What's green, grey and
dangerous?
A toad with a hand grenade!

What's a toad's favourite flower?
A croak-us!

How do you get warty feet?
Wear open-toad sandals!

What do you get if you cross
a toad with a ferry?
A hopper-craft!

Why did the toad become a
lighthouse keeper?
He liked using the frog-horn!

Where do toads leave
their hats and coats?
In the croak-room!

What's a toad's favourite drink?
Croaka-cola!

Why can't you trust a toad?
It is an amp-FIB-ian!

Ha ha ha!

What is a toad's
favourite movie?
Star Warts!

Ha ha!

What's green and red and moves
at a hundred miles per hour?
A toad in a blender!

Have you ever eaten a toad's eyeball?
The taste is *toad-eye* for!

What's green and warty and
standing at the North Pole?
A toad who really needs a good road map!

Why are toads the best
animals in the world?
They're just toadly awesome!

What goes dot-dash-croak,
dash-dash-croak?
Morse toad.

What's white on the outside
and green on the inside?
A toad sandwich.

What's a toad's favourite sweet?
A lolli-hop!

Ha ha ha!

What's a toad's favourite ballet?
Swamp Lake!

How did the toad die?
He simply croaked.

Dad Mum Aunty

Verdigris Horace

Shouty Little Toads!

I'm afraid I can't put it off any longer! I must tell you the tale of Horace and Verdigris Rattlechain: two of the nastiest, noisiest, waste-of-spaciest little toads you could ever hope to avoid.

These twins were very noisy. EXTREMELY noisy. I SHOULD REALLY TELL YOU THE WHOLE OF THIS STORY IN BIG BLACK CAPITAL LETTERS TO MAKE YOU UNDERSTAND JUST HOW NOISY THEY WERE. But I shan't, because shouting so much and for so long without consideration for others would make me no better than they are.

Also, I have a bit of a sore throat today.

However, if you would like to YELL THIS STORY OUT

LOUD through a MEGAPHONE plugged into A VERY LARGE AMPLIFIER with EVEN LARGER SPEAKERS then . . . don't! Honestly, didn't you hear what I just said?

Making an awful racket is an awful racket to be into.

That, however, didn't stop the Rattlechains.

You see, everyone in that whole family was noisy. It was as if, one unfortunate day, they had all had loudspeakers shoved down their throats. Mrs Rattlechain, Mr Rattlechain, Horace, Verdigris and Aunty Lil (their mum's sister) all lived in a house in the middle of a terrace in a once-quiet part of a once-even-quieter town.

And from morning and all through the night, they were NOISY.

Let's take a typical day in the life of the Rattlechains.

The day began at eight o'clock when Mrs Rattlechain woke up. Pale and thin and with thick pink hair, she looked like a stick of candy floss with a mouth big enough to eat herself.

She turned to what appeared to be a large pile of snoring pyjamas beside her. In fact, this was her husband, Bert.

'BERT!' Mrs Rattlechain screeched. 'ARE YOU AWAKE?'

'NO, I'M NOT!' he bellowed back. The two of them laughed with a noise like an old motorcycle being kick-started by an elephant with whooping cough.

'WHAT'S THAT YOU SAID?' shrieked Aunty Lil from the spare room.

Mrs Rattlechain raised her voice to a level that could start avalanches in Nepal. 'I SAID, ARE YOU AWAKE?'

'NO, I'M NOT!' Aunty Lil screamed back.

Well, that started even more laughter, until the walls were shaking and the windows wobbled like grimy glass jellies.

And the Rattlechains' poor neighbours, who already had half a bag of cotton wool stuffed into their earholes, fumbled for the other half and shoved that in too.

One or two tried banging on the wall or yelling at the noisy lot to keep it down. A couple more wished that lightning would strike the Rattlechains' house and blow them all to bits. But in their hearts they knew that this noise wasn't really so bad, and would soon stop – for as long as it was daylight, anyway.

So far, *you* have not heard from Horace and Verdigris. Not a peep.

Perhaps you are thinking, *How could these children NOT be toads, living with such horrible, noisy adults?*

If you are thinking this, please don't.

Because, you see, the children didn't grow toadish because of the parents (and Aunty Lil). The parents (and Aunty Lil) grew toadish because of the *children*.

They *had* to get louder, just to be heard. And with all Horace and Verdigris' din going on each night, their poor battered ears closed up – which meant they had to shout even louder.

After many years, they were now able to sleep through the children's bad behaviour, even if the neighbours couldn't.

'Verdigris,' Horace caterwauled close to midnight.
'Have you heard the story of the headless horseman and the
bottomless horse?'

'No, I haven't, Horace,' she hollered back. 'What's it
about?'

'A headless horseman and a bottomless horse, duh!'
Horace boomed. 'They lost these body parts in a gruesome
accident a hundred years ago when they jumped over a
fence and fell into a combine harvester . . .'

'RUBBISH!' spluttered Verdigris.

'It's true!' Horace called. 'And the man's head and the
horse's bum were stuffed and put in a museum, and every
night the man and the horse ride around the museum
looking for their long-lost head and bum . . .'

'They've had a hundred years to find them,' sneered
Verdigris. 'What's taking them so long? The horse has got
eyes, hasn't it?'

'Um, no! It was a blind horse,' Horace reasoned. 'That's
why it ran into the combine harvester in the first place.'

'SHUT UP!' Verdigris roared. 'Why would the horseman
be dumb enough to ride a blind horse?'

'DUH!' Horace bawled. 'The headless horseman had no
brain, did he?'

'You said he lost his head when the horse ran into the
combine harvester!'

'Yeah, but his brain had already fallen out. It was an

awful accident that happened to him the same day that the horse lost its eyes. They, er . . .'

'Yeah? What? What happened to them?'

'They, um . . .'

'WHAT? WHAT HAPPENED?'

'THEY RODE INTO ANOTHER COMBINE HARVESTER!'

'SHUT UP, THEY NEVER!!'

'SHUT UP, THEY DID!'

The story – and the arguing – went on, at top volume, for hours. The angry neighbours telephoned the police, but the police could do nothing – mostly because they were listening to loud music to drown out the twins' commotion, so they couldn't hear the phone ringing.

After telling their spooky tales, the twins wound up wrestling in the living room. Verdigris scored an early victory when she broke the coffee table with Horace's

head, but Horace was declared overall winner when he left Verdigris wearing the cocktail cabinet.

The contest was fairly noisy. Neighbours banged on the front door in an attempt to complain, until neighbours from further down the street shouted at them to stop because they were only adding to the pandemonium.

After the wrestling, the twins spent a restful hour screaming rude jokes at each other.

VERDIGRIS: What's red, smells and is picked in the garden?

HORACE: *Dunno.*

VERDIGRIS: YOUR BUM!

Hahahahahahahahahahaha!

Their laughter, whether the joke was funny or not (and it rarely was), was like the jibber-jabber of a mad howler monkey trying to swallow a kazoo.

It was *extremely* noisy.

Then the twins would trample around the house playing their favourite games – such as Hide and Seek and

Set Off a Fire Alarm, Throw a Chair Through a Window and Seek, Break Twenty Milk Bottles on the Kitchen Floor and Hide, Hide and Blow Up the Cupboard Under the Stairs and many more – *incredibly* noisily.

After that it was almost five o'clock in the morning – so the twins decided to make a pre-breakfast smoothie of ice cubes, kiwi fruit and Shredded Wheat using Aunty Lil's blender on its loudest setting, and chose to pass the long, ear-hammering minutes with a terrifying karaoke version of that week's number one cranked up to top volume. Then they gulped down the smoothies, held a brief Who Can Belch Loudest? competition and finally conked out on the bedroom floor around six-thirty.

Every night it was the same. Yelling, shouting, singing, howling, charging, thumping, thundering, jumping, exploding, lumbering – upstairs, downstairs, on the stairs ... doing just as they pleased without a thought for the poor souls around them dreaming of sleep.

You might wonder how on earth Horace and Verdigris managed to keep awake at school after misbehaving so badly all through the night.

The answer is, they didn't.

They went to school for a rest!

The terrible twins shuffled through the school doors like zombies, pale and swaying and stumbling about. Their

green eyes were red. The bags under their eyes were more like suitcases.

And so, understandably, Horace and Verdigris slept through their lessons.

They slept in the playground.

They slept in the dinner hall *ZZZ ZZZ*
They slept in their dinner. *ZZZ ZZZ*

The teachers let them sleep too, because Horace and Verdigris were far less trouble when they were snoring. 'Don't rattle the Rattlechains' chains!' they all agreed, for when the Rattlechains were awake they would fidget and fiddle and TALK VERY LOUDLY. The only time Horace and Verdigris ever put up their hands in class was to bellow, 'NEED THE TOILET, SEE YA!!!' so loudly that the classroom windows sometimes cracked.

Yes, the teachers were very glad to let these toadish children push out zeds in the classroom. They woke at the end of each school day quite refreshed, and ready to stay up all night long . . .

While the three-quarters-deafened Mr and Mrs Rattlechain (and Aunty Lil) fell asleep without too much bother, their neighbours were not so lucky. And nor

were their neighbours' neighbours. Or their neighbours'
neighbours' neighbours. Horace and Verdigris' house was
in the middle of a terrace, you may recall, and their noise
travelled clear through the brickwork from house to house
until everyone in the district was woken by the racket.

Everyone – and every*thing*.

Now, I'm going to tell you a secret.

Beyond the Rattlechains' street stretched another
street, and at the end of that street there wound an avenue,
and in the avenue stood an old church and behind the old
church lay a wild and overgrown graveyard. And in the far
corner of the wild and overgrown graveyard was a big, wet,
smelly compost heap.

That's not the secret.

This is:

At the bottom of the big, wet, smelly compost heap
there lived a big, wet, smelly MONSTER.

The monster was fat and slimy and red as rhubarb.
He had been conjured up by accident one dark and stormy
night by some silly old witches who were useless at casting
spells. (They were trying to summon the spirit of an old
Italian mobster, but got an old Italian *monster* instead.
Don't ask. It's a long story.) They went on to throw the poor
monster out of their horrible house! Since it was a long way
from Italy, it went to live in that old, forgotten graveyard,
far from human eyes.

This Italian monster had three tiny eyes, three
twitching claws, three stumpy legs, three stinky feet, two
gaping mouths each with a hundred needle-sharp teeth . . .
And one very large, extremely sensitive ear.

Night after night, when trying to sleep after a slap-up
midnight feast of slugs and pizza crusts, the monster would
toss and turn, unable to rest for the distant rumble of Horace
and Verdigris' night-time noise. Italian monsters are well
known for their patience and kindness (and horrible eating
habits), and this one ignored the disturbance for as long
as possible. But as the sleepless nights turned to sleepless

weeks, and sleepless weeks turned to sleepless months, the monster grew grumpier. And crosser. And meaner.

Until . . .

Verdigris was telling Horace the story of a ghostly alien missile, with excruciating sound effects: 'It haunted whole cities, right, and scared everyone by blowing itself up at midnight. *K4-K4-B00000000000M*!'

'I bet that alien missiles don't go *K4-K4-B00000000000M*!' Horace bellowed. 'They go *KKKKKKKKKKRRRRRR00000000000000000M*!'

'Not GHOSTLY ones,' Verdigris screamed in his face. 'GHOSTLY ones go *K4-K4-B00000000000M* because they have, like, undead alien exploding crystals in them.'

'THEY DO NOT!' Horace spat.

'THEY DO SO TOO!' Verdigris spat back. 'And when everyone in the city saw the ghostly explosion they went, "*YARRRRRRRRRRRRGH*—!" just like that.'

'THEY NEVER!'

'THEY DID! YOU DON'T KNOW!'

'I DO KNOW, AND THEY NEVER.'

'THEY DID, THEY WENT, "*YARRRRRRRRRRRRGHHHHHHHH*!"'

'YOU SAID THEY ONLY WENT, "*YARRRRRRRRRRRRGH*!"'

'THEY WENT, "*YARRRRRRRRRRRRGH*!" THE FIRST TIME THE GHOSTLY ALIEN MISSILE WENT *K4-K4-*

BOOOOOOOOOOOM, AND "*YARRRRRRRRRRRRGHHHHHHHH*!"
THE SECOND TIME—'

'THEY NEVER, AND I TOLD YOU
IT'S NOT *KA-KA-BOOOOOOOOOOOM*! IT'S
KKKKKKKKKKRRRRRROOOOOOOOOOOOOOOOOM!'

'IT IS *NOT*!!!'

Even by the
Rattlechains' standards,
this was a super noisy
night. The house was
shaking so hard it
threatened to collapse and

bring
down
the rest of the street
with it. Mr and Mrs
Rattlechain stirred
in their sleep, and
Aunty Lil snarled
in her snoring. The
neighbours were

beating on the walls
and the neighbours'
neighbours were sobbing
in their beds, and the
neighbours' neighbours'

neighbours were shouting and wailing things that are far too rude to write down here.

That was when the monster in the wild, overgrown graveyard crawled out from the compost and decided to take matters into its own three hands.

'*Sono arrabbiato!*' it snarled in Italian, which, if you snarl it in English, means, 'I'm angry!'

It thumped and rumbled – or *thrumbled* – out of the graveyard, past the old church, along the avenue and down the street on its three scuttling legs. It could move very quickly when it wanted to. It homed in on the dreadful racket like a noise-seeking monstery missile. And this monster was not ghostly at all. It was solid and real and *rabbioso* . . .

The monster had already eaten a fine amount of slugs that night.

Now it was hungry for something more . . .

You might say that HORRID NOISY TOADS were on its menu!

The louder the Rattlechains' noise grew in its sensitive ear, the madder the monster became. It thrumbled past the neighbours and the police. It thrumbled up to Horace and Verdigris' front door and its eyes narrowed to tiny slits. With a snap of its blood-red jaws, its teeth sprang out to their fullest and scariest extent.

Then the monster raised its three clawed fists and

– **BLAM! BLAM! BLAM!** – knocked on the door so hard it smashed it off its hinges.

Horace and Verdigris, still screaming at each other in their bedroom, heard the splintering crash and – incredibly – fell silent.

They listened. Hard.

All they could hear were the snores and snuffles of their parents in bed and the dreamland mutterings of Aunty Lil in the spare room. The ticking of a clock. The hum of the fridge. Comforting noises of home, noises that said everything was fine. Noises, sadly, that they had never before been able to hear over all the ruckus and row they made. Not until this very moment.

Only, as they heard the monster downstairs lick its thick leathery lips and hiss like a hundred snakes as it stepped inside the house, they knew that everything was not fine. Not even a little bit.

'MUM! DAD!' yelled Horace and Verdigris together. 'AUNTY LIL!'

But the adults would not wake. They were far too used to horrible noises to stir even for a second.

The monster, meanwhile, thrumbled boldly up the stairs.

Now the twins could hear the rasp of its breathing . . . the scratch of its toenails on every step . . . the scrape of its claws on the wallpaper. These were *not* comforting noises.

Horace looked at Verdigris. Verdigris looked at Horace . . .

They turned and stared as the monster appeared in their bedroom doorway. They clung together as it raised its arms and widened its mouth in all its petrifying, gory, tooth-and-clawy glory. They opened their mouths to scream for help – but, as if caught in a nightmare, they found that not a whisper left their lips. The twins were so scared, they couldn't make a sound! They could warn no one of their predicament: not that anyone would have paid attention to another scream from the Rattlechains in any case . . .

Luckily for Horace and Verdigris, one look at the twins was enough to convince the monster they would give it indigestion for a month. Instead, just ahead of creeping back

to the comforts of its compost heap, the monster carefully folded over its sensitive ear and HOWLED.

A *hurricane* of a HOWL. A humungous, horrifying, head-hammering HOWL so dreadful it shattered the windows and turned brickwork to putty. As their bedroom blew away about them, Horace and Verdigris were sent tumbling into the night . . .

Mum and Dad and Aunty Lil woke a little earlier than usual next day. It was chilly in the house, mainly because their second-biggest bedroom was now scattered up and down the street.

And so too were Horace and Verdigris.

Mr and Mrs Rattlechain pottered outside to retrieve

their children. The
twins looked different:
their hair had turned
white with fright. And,
strangely, they sounded
rather different too.

Neither Horace nor
Verdigris could say a word.
The poor revolting toads! That vengeful monster had not
just scared them silly – it had scared them *dumb*.

The twins were taken to the doctor, but there wasn't
much he could do besides hand out celebratory cigars to
everyone else in the neighbourhood. For, after the eyebrow-
raising events of that fateful night, neither Horace nor
Verdigris were able to utter or stutter a single syllable.

Don't feel too bad for them. It took a very long time, but
I'm afraid their voices did come back in . . .

The End

Spoiled Little Toad!

Do the people who look after you ever give you treats? I'm sure they do. If you've been well behaved on a trip to the supermarket, perhaps they get you some sweets. Or on a trip to town, you might get a toy to play with – even if it's not your birthday. Or if you tidy your room, or help in the garden, or make a special effort not to scribble all over your little sister with felt-tip pens, you might just get a reward.

I'm sure your pet grown-ups have told you that it is good to share things too. You know, grown-ups are extremely impressed when a child shares something they like with their brother or sister, or with a friend. This sort of behaviour is almost guaranteed to get praise, or perhaps

a treat. The sensible child will practise sharing right away although you probably shouldn't do it all the time, because a) grown-ups will get used to it and stop being impressed or b) they might think the real you has been stolen by aliens and that a perfectly perfect robot replica has taken your place. There have been several UFO sightings lately, you know – do take care, won't you?)

In any case, some children behave very badly, never share a single thing and still expect treats. They behave very, VERY badly and, if they don't get what they want, their behaviour grows even worse.

Take Jeremiah Bratson, for instance.

If only somebody would!

Look at him, in his fancy-pants suit with his nose in the air. He was a proper spoiled little toad.

Jeremiah's mother and father were terribly wealthy. By which I mean, wealth had made them terrible. They had made a fortune from making and selling all sorts of vehicles from sports cars to space rockets, and now spent most of their time racing round the south of France in a Ferrari. It only had two seats, so Jeremiah was left at home with a nanny – and the most overstocked playroom in the world.

The nanny was under strict instructions to give Jeremiah any treat he wanted.

'Jeremiah simply must have more toys, more games, more everything than anyone else,' said Mrs Bratson. 'See to it!'

Mr Bratson nodded keenly. 'Only the best is good enough for a Bratson!'

And so the nanny, whose name was Kevin, took Jeremiah to the poshest toy stores in the city. Kevin took a shopping trolley – and Jeremiah took everything in the shop that wasn't nailed down. As they paraded around, Jeremiah tried to hold on to all the toys, even ones he already had . . . even ones he didn't like. At the end of the trip he would perch on top of the teetering toy-pile in the trolley, clinging to his latest loot and resolving not to share it with anyone in the world.

'It's mine!' he cried, clutching greedily for more and more. 'Give me! Give me! It's mine!' He sobbed and screamed, 'NOT FAIR!' when the person at the till had to pick them up to scan them.

What a miserable, spoiled little brat!

When he got home, Jeremiah would rip open the toy boxes, spend a minute or so playing with each thing, and then toss it over his shoulder and tear open the next. Kevin watched sadly. The toy room was the size of a palace, but one day soon it would be full.

'What happens when there's no more room in here, Jeremiah?' Kevin asked.

'Duh!' Jeremiah threw another toy over his shoulder. 'Mama and Papa will buy me a NEW playroom, stupid!'

'I suppose they will,' said Kevin. How he hated his job!

'What do you want to do tomorrow?'

Jeremiah narrowed his eyes. 'I want all the neighbourhood children to come over.'

'That's so nice of you, Jeremiah!' Kevin was quite shocked. 'It will be fun to share your toys.'

'Share? ARE YOU CRAZY?' Jeremiah screeched. 'I'm inviting them round to *watch* me play – but if anyone tries to touch one of my toys they'll be chucked out at once!'

'Oh, dear,' sighed Kevin. There was certainly little chance of him believing that aliens had replaced Jeremiah Bratson with a perfectly perfect robot replica! If anything, he might have believed that aliens had replaced Jeremiah with an even nastier version. But, no.

It was just the way Jeremiah was.

Next day, loads of children came to visit – and I'm afraid that Jeremiah was as good as his word.

'Come in. Sit down. Shut up,' he snapped, then pulled a vast sheet off the enormous pile of gifts he'd received the day before. 'It's your lucky day! Here is a large pile of presents, all for me. You may stay and applaud me while I play with them. Isn't that super?'

With that, he began to throw his gifts about, giddily gloating and giggling over his horde of loot. Some of the visiting children tried to pick up the toys he discarded, but Jeremiah chased them off like a mad guard dog. 'No!' he snarled, snatching each toy back. 'It's mine! Give me! Give me! It's mine!'

Not surprisingly, the children soon decided to leave.

'How rude they are!' cried Jeremiah, as the front door closed behind them. 'Ungrateful goats!'

'They were bored,' Kevin told him. 'You didn't let them play with anything. You didn't share a single thing!'

'Of course not! These are *my* toys!' Jeremiah pulled a face. 'Where have those rude children gone? What could possibly be better than watching me enjoy myself?'

Almost anything on earth, thought Kevin, *and anything on any other planet, I'm sure*! He stared out of the window. People had reported mysterious lights in the sky around the place lately, and Kevin almost hoped that aliens from outer space might beam him up to a better place.

'Look,' he said, pointing to the children as they made their way towards the park down the hill. 'They're going to the playground instead.'

'Why?' asked Jeremiah, flabbergasted.

Kevin smiled. 'Perhaps because the playground belongs to everyone, so everyone can play.'

'*Everyone* can play?' Jeremiah sneered. 'Well, we'll soon see about that!' He selected one of the thirteen new smartphones lying around his playroom. 'I am going to have a private phone call with my mama, Kevin. Go away.'

'With pleasure,' Kevin muttered, and left the room.

Jeremiah called his mother's phone and lowered his voice. 'Hello, Mama.'

'Who's that?' asked Mrs Bratson.

'It's your son.'

'Who?'

'Jeremiah. You know: nine years old, blond hair, lives in your house—'

'Oh, yes, I remember now. Well, what do you want? I'm very busy finding out how many diamonds it takes to bury a double-decker bus.'

'Never mind that, Mama. Go and fetch your credit card!' Jeremiah smiled slyly. 'I want you to do something for me right away . . .'

*

The following day, the children went to the playground again – but they were in for a nasty shock.

Signs had been put up saying KEEP OUT and PRIVATE PROPERTY and NOT FOR YOU! Barbed wire surrounded the playground. There was even a sentry box made of wood in front of the gate – and as the children stared in dismay, a figure stepped out from inside.

It was, of course, Jeremiah Bratson.

Do you know what he'd done? Jeremiah had persuaded his mother to BUY the playground. She'd paid a small fortune for it – well, quite a big fortune actually.

And now it belonged to Jeremiah, and to make sure everyone knew, he squawked through a loudhailer. 'These are my rides now! You may stay and watch me play with them all!'

'Can't we play too?' a boy asked.

'You can't ride on everything at once,' a girl added.

'They're right, Jeremiah,' said Kevin firmly. 'These rides were meant to be shared, and that's what you're going to do.' He pushed aside the sentry box and held open the gate. 'Come on, children, in you come.'

'NO! STOP!' Jeremiah wailed as the children pushed past. 'This playground is MINE, not theirs!' He ran around, pulling children off the roundabout and pushing them off the swings. 'It's mine! Give me!' Faster and faster he went, kicking them off the monkey bars and bumping them off the balance beams. 'Give me! It's mine!'

'You've gone too far, Jeremiah!' Kevin ran up to the horrible toad, determined to stop him. Alas, Jeremiah jumped on to one end of the seesaw and the other end swung up and socked Kevin on the chin. Kevin went cross-eyed and fell over backwards.

'Kevin, you are fired!' Jeremiah shouted in triumph, as the other children ran to fetch help. 'Now, I'm going to phone Mama and tell her to buy this whole town for me. I'll kick everyone out of their houses and take all their toys for myself – that will teach them!'

However, while Jeremiah patted his pockets in pursuit of his phone, he didn't see the strange sight overhead.

You see, the people who'd spotted mysterious, glowing alien spaceships in the sky were absolutely RIGHT. And just then, one came floating down silently from the sky, to land softly beside the climbing frame.

Jeremiah didn't notice the two big green alien monsters lumber out.

'We have found him!'

the first big green alien monster cried. 'After searching for so long, we have finally found the nastiest person on Planet Earth – just as our children wanted.'

The second big green alien monster pulled a funny gadget from a pouch in its belly – something like a camera crossed with a gun. 'Say "squeee", little human . . .'

Jeremiah turned round – and his eyes nearly popped out of his head. 'SQUEEEEEEEEEEE!' he screamed as the second alien shone a blue light all over him.

'There!' the second alien said. 'All scanned and ready for replacement.'

'No one else can say they own the nastiest human on this world,' said the first big green alien monster proudly. 'He will make a fitting pet for our nasty little ones.'

'L-l-little ones?' Jeremiah squeaked.

A moment later, the two nasty little ones (who were each easily as big as an armchair) came squelching out of the spaceship with a look of pure joy on their unusual faces.

Jeremiah turned to run, but it was too late. One of the little ones grabbed his arms and the other little one grabbed his legs. They pulled Jeremiah this way and that way like big green alien dogs with a tug toy.

'Give me!' gurgled one.

'It's mine!' grunted the other. 'Give ME.'

'It's mine!' giggled the first.

'Let go of me!' squealed Jeremiah, his face squashed in an alien armpit. 'Put me down, I beg you!'

'Don't listen to him, boys,' said the first big green alien monster. 'He never cared about other people's feelings, so you don't have to care about his!'

The second big green alien monster carried a robot out of the spaceship, laid it on the grass and fired its scanner again.

In a snap, the robot became a perfect double of Jeremiah Bratson!

'We've done this planet a great favour,' said the second big green alien monster happily. 'I'm sure the humans will find this robot a great improvement on the original . . .'

'You can't do this to me!' Jeremiah raged as the big green alien monster family whisked him away on to their spaceship. 'I'm too rich! I'm too handsome! Release me at once!'

'Mine!' cried the first little one.

'Mine!' cried the second.

A few moments later, the spaceship took off, and disappeared into the sky.

✳

Soon after that, Kevin the nanny groaned and opened his eyes. He had a big bruise on his chin. A doctor was standing over him, along with several concerned children and their parents.

'Don't try to get up,' said the doctor. 'You've had a nasty bump.'

'I'm so sorry, Kevin,' said a familiar voice behind him. 'From now on I will be truly grateful for every gift I receive, I will share everything and I will never behave so horribly ever again.'

Kevin looked up dizzily, and frowned. 'Jeremiah?!'

The familiar face smiled back at him. It looked like Jeremiah. It sounded like Jeremiah. But how on earth,

Kevin thought, could the boy have changed so suddenly . . .
so completely?

He smiled. It was almost as if the real Jeremiah had
been stolen by aliens and a perfectly perfect robot replica
had taken his place . . .

Well, I'm sure those slimy squabbling space aliens will
bring the real Jeremiah back home one day. After all, who
would want to keep hold of such a nasty little toad?

Until then, Kevin the nanny will happily look after
the new, improved Jeremiah, and the children will enjoy
playing with the old Jeremiah's mountain of toys, and those
mysterious lights in the sky will be nowhere to be seen.

That's how life is, I find. Things always come good in . . .

The End

TOAD FACTS

Human toads are horrid, but actual toads are amazing animals! Did you know these twelve true toad-tacular facts?

1) Unlike frogs, toads do not need to live near water to survive.

2) Toads' skin has a bitter taste and smell that keeps many predators away.

3) The collective noun for many toads is a KNOT of toads. (Knot a lot of people know that!)

4) Besides Antarctica, toads can be found on every continent in the world.

5) Toads can eat up to a thousand insects in one day.

6) Toads start life as tadpoles, just like frogs.

7) Toads have to swallow their food whole – they have no teeth so they can't chew.

8) Toads can shed their skin – and when they do, they eat it.

9) Toads hibernate through the winter months.

10) A typical wild toad can live for ten to fifteen years – but a wild toad called Georgie from Hull in the UK lived for over forty years.

11) Toads can breathe through their skin.

12) A female cane toad can lay up to thirty-five thousand eggs at a time, twice a year.

School hating Little Toad!

Have you ever heard of Hermione Sludge? Dreadful girl. Sludge by name and sludge for brains. A most moany and ridiculous toad!

Now, you know me. I firmly feel that it is never too late to change. And yet, in the case of Hermione Sludge, I'm not so sure.

Perhaps if I tell you her story, you can judge for yourself.

Hermione was one of those children who moaned about school and everything to do with it.

Now, I'm sure you have moaned about school as well, particularly when you have a lot of homework, or on a Sunday night when the school week stretches ahead of you.

That's fine. You'd be most unusual if you *didn't* moan. Still, at the end of the day, moaning doesn't change anything – school is a fact of life.

But a fact of Hermione Sludge is that she moaned about school ALL of the time.

'I hate the lessons!' she whined. 'I hate my teachers! I hate homework! I hate my school uniform!'

There was no reasoning with her. Goodness knows, her dad tried.

'I hate my school bag!' shrieked Hermione one Monday morning.

'Well, pet,' said Mr Sludge, 'we'll get you a new school bag.'

'No, I'd hate that one too!' she wailed. 'And I hate walking to school!'

'Why, then, I'll drive you.'

'I hate driving to school!'

'You could take your bike?'

'I hate cycling to school!'

Mr Sludge gritted his teeth. 'All right, then, we'll stuff you into a giant medieval catapult and fire you in the direction of school.'

Hermione considered for a moment. 'That actually sounds pretty good except for the *boring old school* part. WHYYYYYYYYYY do I have to go to school?'

'Well, you have to learn, my pet.'

'I *hate* learning!' Hermione bawled. 'It's not fair! Kids in the old days NEVER went to school.'

'You only know *that* because you learned it at school,' Mr Sludge pointed out.

'HOW DARE YOU?' Hermione looked appalled. 'I SAW IT ON TV!'

Wearily, Mr Sludge dragged his dismal daughter out of the house and off to school. Every step fetched a fresh ridiculous whine from her lips:

'I hate my coat peg, it's too high! I hate the whiteboard markers, they aren't scented!' Hermione raised her voice. 'I wish I could go back in time to when kids were lucky – to when there *was* no school!'

This, dear reader, was a rash wish to make. I trust that you will take care should you ever make an unwise wish yourself.

Because, you see, you never know who might be listening.

As it happens, one of my colleagues in the witching world was close by – an unpleasant old trout by the name of Wanda Nemetrix. She was one of the witches who, you may remember, summoned the poor Italian monster that badly scared Horace and Verdigris Rattlechain! As Hermione was dragged to school, Wanda was tramping through someone's back garden in search of Eye of Newt. Just as she found it, she heard Hermione's heartfelt plea from beyond the bushes.

Wanda – who resembles a wart that has grown a body without reading the instructions first – is no great fan of children, particularly toady ones, and immediately decided to involve herself in the situation.

'Is that what you wish for?' Wanda cackled. 'Then I think it's high time someone taught you a lesson. Your wish shall be GRANTED!' She leaned out from the bushes, snatched a strand of Hermione's hair, and slunk back home, chuckling.

Wanda got busy, threading Hermione's hair through the Eye of Newt. Then she plopped it in a cauldron along with several other extremely dodgy ingredients and was soon casting a spirited and spectacular spell of time travel . . .

Hermione had been moaning her way through lunch and was the last to come stomping down the corridor to her classroom. As she opened the door, the spell took effect. She felt dizzy, as if the whole school stood on a merry-go-round and was starting to spin, and rise, and fall, and rise . . .

'Stupid school,' Hermione mumbled as she staggered into the classroom. Then she stopped with a gasp.

Her classroom was empty. No pupils, no teacher. It suddenly looked different, like a Victorian dining room, cold and draughty with an enormous fireplace on one wall.

'Huh?' Hermione stared, scratching her head. 'I must've come in through the wrong door. What is this place?'

'Oi!' came a chirpy voice from the fireplace. "Scuse me, miss, are you the one what's been moaning about school?'

Hermione frowned. 'Who wants to know?'

'I do!' A sooty face appeared from inside the fireplace and made Hermione jump. It was a scrawny young boy's face with bright blue eyes. 'I'm a chimney sweep, see? I heard you ain't happy.'

'I'm not happy because school is the worst thing in the world and I hate it.' Hermione tore her eyes from the skinny boy and glanced quickly around. 'Although, right now, I must be asleep and dreaming, because I'm talking to you and the whole school seems to have vanished.'

'There's no school here.' The filthy, stick-thin sweep swaggered up to her in a cloud of soot. 'This is 1818. I've been squeezed up chimneys cleaning 'em since I was five.' He shrugged. 'Still, I'm sure you have it worse, having to go to *school.*'

'Oh, MUCH worse.' Hermione nodded gravely. 'They make us sit down all day and *learn* things . . .'

'D'you wanna swap with me?' cried the sweep.

'Swap?' Hermione thought hard. *I'll never have to go to school again! I'll never have to put up with Dad's moaning about how ungrateful I am! I can stay here and earn money in an actual job! What a kind and generous sweep to make such an offer!*

'Yes! Yes, I'll swap with you!' Hermione clapped her hands. 'But how do we make that happen?'

'Easy-peasy!' A different voice came from the fireplace – a rasping, grating cackle of a voice . . . the voice of Wanda the witch! 'I'll just do a swift spell of life-swapping . . . and then YOU'LL do a long spell of hard labour, Hermione Sludge!

'**Girl with brains like empty space:
BOOM! This boy will take your place!**'

Hermione felt dizzy again. She heard the sweep cheering and for a moment she thought she saw him, sitting in her place in the classroom, holding up his hand to answer a question.

'Toodles!' cooed Wanda behind her.

There was a flash of dazzling green light. Hermione blinked and found a fierce, red-faced man standing over her with a long spiky brush.

'What're you staring at me for?' he snarled. 'I'm your master, and I don't want any cheek from you. You'll start on a penny a week.'

Hermione boggled. 'One penny a *week*?'

'I know, I'm spoiling you. Now, go on, get working! WORK!'

And so began a horrendous new chapter in Hermione's life. She had a dreadful, dirty, muscle-aching, bone-breaking, soot-spitting life squashed up in chimneys, and all for a penny a week!

The monstrous master got fed up of Hermione's moaning before long, and sacked her. (By which I mean he hit her with a sack.) Hermione decided she would quit the job and strike out on her own.

Well, not *quite* on her own. That wicked Wanda Nemetrix was keeping an eye on the poor toad, and she had more mischief in mind.

Not long after sweeping away her life as a sweep, Hermione was looking for shelter. She wandered into a coal mine; or rather she *Wanda'd* into it, for the witch had secretly steered her there, and was ready for some more fun at Hermione's expense.

Hermione entered a dark tunnel that sloped down, down, down, lit dimly by lanterns hooked to the wall. The tunnel got narrower and narrower, the roof got lower and lower, the temperature dropped colder and colder. The air was thick with coal dust.

'Hello?' came a distant voice from the darkness. 'Is that the girl who hates school?'

Hermione hurried forwards and, finally, in the light of a tiny, sputtering candle, she saw a girl her age, thin as a twig and coated in dust, sitting beside a wooden door holding on to a piece of string.

'How did you know me?' Hermione asked. 'Who are you?'

'I'm a trapper, aren't I?' The girl tugged on her string and the wooden door creaked open. 'When I hear the coal truck coming down the rails, I open this door to let it through and close it straight after. I wish I could go to a proper school, like you did.'

'Then you're silly,' snapped Hermione. 'What else do you do?'

'Nothing,' said the girl. 'Just that, for a shilling a day.'

She just sits here all day! thought Hermione. *And a shilling a day is RICHES compared to one penny a week.* 'What an easy life!' Hermione cried. 'I wish I could just sit around all day like you!'

'Perhaps I can help again?' boomed Witch Wanda from the shadows. 'Hermione Sludge, you have a choice: you can either go back to school, or swap places with the trapper.'

'I'm never going back to school!' said Hermione. 'I *will* swap places with this girl here.'

'It's a miracle!' The girl leaped up with joy. She banged her head on the tunnel roof but even that couldn't wipe the smile from her face.

Wanda cackled nastily and chanted her spell:

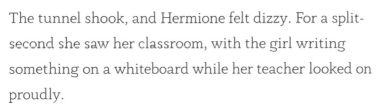

**'Girl with brains like empty space,
Now this trapper takes your place!'**

The tunnel shook, and Hermione felt dizzy. For a split-second she saw her classroom, with the girl writing something on a whiteboard while her teacher looked on proudly.

'Toodles!' Wanda waved.

There was a green flash. Hermione blinked, and found herself sitting in the shadowy dark beside the door, holding the string, in the feeble candlelight.

'Easy life,' she told herself.

But it was not.

Hermione soon found that a trapper had to sit on her own in the dark for twelve hours a day, six days a week.

She had to sleep in the girl's tiny
house with five other children
and rise before the sun to reach
the coal mine by five-thirty in the
morning. She had no one to talk to
all day. A piece of stale bread for
lunch. When Hermione finally got
home and blew her nose it was like
a dirty fire extinguisher going off
and filled the room with soot.

  In the end, she got fed up.
'There must be something better I can do . . .'
  She wandered (and *Wanda*'d) here, there and
everywhere in search of a better life – better than school,
and better than being a chimney sweep or a trapper.
  Wanda was happy to help her out.
  'You may go back to school, or swap places with
a matchstick dipper,' Wanda
declared.

'A matchstick dipper
– that sounds nice and easy,'
said Hermione. 'Let me swap
with her!'
  So she did. And it was
dreadful. She worked sixteen
hours a day in a hot, cramped

factory, dipping wood into jars of phosphorus before cutting them into matchsticks. The phosphorus fumes made her breath blue and her sick glow in the dark. The girl she'd swapped with much preferred the smell of school dinners and wearing a clean school uniform!

'You may go back to school, or swap places with a mudlark,' Wanda decreed.

'I'll NEVER go back to school,' Hermione spat (and very alarming her spit was too, being bright yellow and highly toxic). 'You're trying to trick me. A mudlark? Anything with "lark" in its name must be fun!'

Sadly, it was not.

A mudlark had to hunt through mud and sewage along the banks of a city river for anything they could find and sell. Hermione mostly found dead cats and broken glass.

Time and again she swapped places, determined that she should not be tricked into going back to school. 'Anything's better than school,' Hermione told herself, over and over. 'Anything!'

Wanda Nemetrix had expected her little toad to crack and croak off back to the classroom long before now. It was no longer such fun, finding poor Victorian children to swap places with Hermione.

Finally, while working as a leech collector in a filthy marsh, with bloodsucking blobs all over her arms and legs, Hermione reached the conclusion that perhaps school had NOT been, after all, quite so bad.

'I was wrong!' she bellowed. 'I want to go to school, I want to go!'

Wanda popped up beside her and smiled. 'You do? Well, that's splendid news. I'll take you back at once!'

'Oh, thank you!' cried Hermione, pulling a fat, black leech from her leg. 'School, here I come. How about that? I actually want a lesson!'

'I've been teaching you a lesson for quite some time,' said Wanda with a smile. She reversed her spell at long last and Hermione felt herself fading away, through time and space . . .

The journey ended in a flash of yellow light. Rain was falling on a cool September morning. Hermione was standing in front of her old school, as pupils hurried up the path to the playground. It looked somewhat smaller than before.

'I'm here!' she cried. 'It's happened! I'm really going to school!'

'Are you?' One of the pupils stopped and looked up at her. 'Are you a new teacher?'

'Teacher?' Hermione spluttered. 'Don't be stupid. I'm like you, I'm only a . . . child?'

She looked down at the puddle by her feet and saw her reflection. It was the reflection of a grown-up young lady.

Poor Hermione! She had wasted so many years trying all those different jobs that it was now WAY too late for her to catch up with her schoolwork!

Still, you know, Wanda Nemetrix knows a thing or two about turning back time – I'm sure she'll roll Hermione back a few years to leave her the same age as before: if the moaning little toad has learned her lesson.

But I hope that *you* will learn a lesson from Hermione not learning a lesson about learning lessons.

Class dismissed! School for the day has reached . . .

The End

Unhealthy Little Toads!

'Eat up your greens!'

'No chocolate before you've had some fruit!'

'If you're not main-course hungry, you're not pudding hungry!'

'Sorry, tomato ketchup does not count as one of your five a day!'

Have you ever heard these words, or words like them, burst from the mouths of those looking after you?

Of course you have!

It's a sad fact of life that none of us can eat exactly what we want.

97

You might love pizza and chips so much you want to eat them for breakfast, lunch and dinner. But they're salty and oily and may make you fat and spotty, so it's a bad idea.

You might adore strawberries and want to guzzle them every minute of the day. But that will leave you with diarrhoea, so it's another bad idea.

The best thing to do is to have a balanced diet: each day you eat some of the things you love, and some of the things you don't like much, but which a) help your body function properly and b) stop grown-ups from hassling you.

Hopefully that's the sort of sensible diet you have.

  But I know a pair of proper toads whose diet is *not* sensible, and neither are they. They are twins and their names are Marco and Rosa Broccoli.

Marco hates vegetables. Rosa hates fruit. Marco hates fruit almost as much as vegetables. Rosa hates vegetables almost as much as fruit.

For them, a typical day's balanced meals consist of:

Breakfast: crisps, chocolate bar, doughnuts (with extra sugar and sprinkles).

Lunch: deep-fried chicken, a hot dog, two bags of crisps, a deep-fried chocolate bar, one large packet of chocolate-chip cookies.

Dinner: pizza stuffed inside a hamburger stuffed inside a pasty. With chips. And pancakes with bacon and syrup. And a fried egg. And ketchup.

They really did eat the most awful things. Their mum didn't mind because she ate what she wanted too. Their house was a no-fruit-and-veg zone.

You might think I'm exaggerating. Well, I'm not.

Once, Marco went to McBurgers and was accidentally served a bag of carrot sticks instead of fries. He got such a shock that he fainted. When he'd recovered, he vowed revenge – and promptly kidnapped an order of cheeseburgers from the drive-in window.

Twice, Rosa got lost in a supermarket and accidentally walked into the fruit aisle. Confronted with so much goodness she ran riot, stamping on kiwi fruits, grapes and blueberries and attempting to strangle a melon before security guards picked her up.

Such overreactions to fruit and vegetables are not normal. But then, Marco and Rosa are not normal children.

On two separate occasions they attempted to sue their mum for not allowing them to change their name from 'Broccoli' to 'Steak-Pie'.

When Marco was introduced to his vegetarian cousin, he attacked her with a pack of mince.

When Rosa was offered an apple to eat, she tried to flush it down the toilet but it jammed in the pipe and flooded the house.

Neither of them can hear a healthy word like 'grape' or 'courgette' without running around screaming.

It should come as no surprise to learn that their favourite time of year was always Halloween. Halloween, when you can go out trick-or-treating for bags full of chocolate and sticky sweets.

For most children, it's a special fun treat.

For Marco and Rosa, it was a chance to scoff more and more sweets and chocolate for free. They took Halloween very seriously. Indeed, they would prepare a variety of different outfits so that they could go out promptly, rush around collecting their treats, rush back home and put on *another* costume, go back out, rush around collecting more treats, rush back home and put on *ANOTHER* costume, go back out, rush around collecting more treats and so on, until they came back sweaty and panting for breath with a ton of candy and scoffed it all for tea, laughing about how clever they were with their mouths full and dirty dribble drooling. Not a pretty sight.

However, last Halloween, things didn't work out quite in the way they wanted.

Because, last Halloween, Marco and Rosa happened to trick-or-treat on the house of a *real* witch.

And that witch happened to be ME.

Now, you know me. As witches go, I'm quite a dear! (I'm MUCH nicer than whiffy Wanda Nemetrix – and so much prettier too!) I'm naturally very fond of Halloween – it's my time of year! I join in with the traditions, giving sweet treats to everyone who calls on my door.

BUT!

I don't like it when people try to trick me to get more than their fair share!

When Marco and Rosa knocked on my door the first time, dressed as demons,

I gave them a generous handful of chocolates.

When they changed into bats and tried knocking a second time, I gave them pieces of cereal bar – less desirable than chocolate, but still sweet and a snack that might actually have done them some good.

But when they changed into devils and tried knocking a third time, I'd had enough.

'I've treated you twice,' I cried. 'Now it's time for a trick!' As Rosa held out her bucket, I dropped a banana in it. As Marco held out his, he received a half-cucumber. 'There you are – *bon appetit!*'

I thought perhaps this tiresome twosome would turn around, accept defeat and slink sheepishly away. But, no.

'You mean old bat!' cried Rosa.

'You should be put in prison,' Marco snarled. 'No one hands out fruit and veg on Halloween.' And with that, he took my perfectly good cucumber and hurled it on to my patio. **SPLAT!** He stamped on it. Then Rosa threw the banana on to my front lawn and jumped up and down on it!

I stared in horror. 'You ungrateful toads! You just squished perfectly good food.'

'Yep!' Rosa leered at me. 'What are you going to do about it, you old witch?'

'An old witch is exactly what I am,' I informed her. 'And I'll tell you what I'm going to do. I'm going to teach you to appreciate fruit and vegetables.'

'Never!' they chorused. 'Never ever!'

'It's never too late to change, children!' I told them with my sweetest smile.

Marco and Rosa didn't believe me, of course. Not then, anyway!

They swaggered away to get the next lot of treats before anyone more deserving could take them.

I stared at the mushed-up cucumber and the banana. They could no longer be eaten, but they wouldn't go to waste.

They would go into a special *spell . . .*

✳

That Halloween night, Rosa and Marco went home with a mountain of sweet treats.

The house was quiet and dark. The lights weren't working. The pale glare of the full moon was all they had to guide them up the stairs to where their mum lay, fast asleep in her bedroom.

'Wake up, Mum!' Marco tapped her. She didn't stir. He shook her. Still she didn't stir. He waved a freshly unwrapped walnut whip under her nose. Still she didn't stir.

(It was almost as if a clever witch had cast a Sleep Without a Peep spell! However did THAT happen? Hee, hee.)

'Never mind Mum,' Rosa said. 'Let's get eating our chocolate feast!' She snatched the walnut whip from Marco's fingers and was about to stuff the whole thing in her mouth when—

'AROOOOOOOOOOOOOOOOOOOOOOO!'

An inhuman, slightly fruity howl came floating up from downstairs. It was a sound to chill the blood and – far more seriously – to knock the walnut whip from a greedy girl's hand.

'What was that?' hissed Marco.

The dark house was silent once more, until, suddenly—

Thump. Thud. Thump.

Something was coming up the stairs.

Thump. Thump. Thud.

It was as if something small and unearthly was hopping from step to step, until – **THUMP** – it reached the landing and – **THUMP, THUD** – it made its unnatural way towards their mum's bedroom.

Rosa and Marco were quaking with fear. They rocked their mum, they jumped on her, they slapped her cheeks (both upper and lower), they yelled in her ears, 'WAKE UPPPPPPP!' but *still* she wouldn't stir!

Then the bedroom door swung open, and in the light of the moon the twins saw . . .

A small, hairy figure. A small, hairy figure that looked strangely like a banana balancing on its tip, but with the fur of a wolf. Mean red eyes glared at Marco and Rosa, and as it howled again it showed spiky teeth.

The figure was part-werewolf, part-banana. In other words . . . a *were-nana!*

Rosa and Marco screamed in horror as the were-nana bounced towards them, teeth bared, red eyes glowing like lasers. They abandoned their mum and ran in panic around the room.

It seemed that everywhere they turned, the were-nana was bouncing before them, blocking the way, howling at the top of its nutritious lungs!

Finally, Marco managed to get out on to the landing. Rosa tried to follow but the were-nana placed its potassium-rich banana booty in front of her feet and she tripped and fell – straight into her twin. Both tumbled down the stairs in a tangle of arms and legs.

THUMP. THUD. THUMP. The were-nana came after them.

Hearts a-hammering, they raced to the front door . . .
only to find a sinister skinny shape rising before them,
mottled and green and dressed only in a black cape with
a red velvet lining. Two enormous fangs protruded from
its blank face, and its wet yellow eyes were narrowed in
hate.

The figure was part-vampire, part-cucumber. In other
words . . . a *vamp-cumber*!

'Trick or treat?' the vamp-cumber cried in a high,
wavery voice.

Rosa gasped. 'It's blocking our way out.'

'Noooooooooo!' wailed Marco.

THUMP. THUD. '**AROOOOOOOOOO**!' The were-nana had
almost reached the bottom of the stairs.

'Quickly, the kitchen door!' Rosa turned and ran, Marco
close behind. 'We'll get out that way.'

But somehow, the vamp-cumber was back, floating in front of them! 'No, no! You can't leave. You haven't had your treat . . . !'

'**AROooooooooooooo**!' the were-nana agreed (probably).

Marco and Rosa pushed past the vamp-cumber and tried the back door. It was locked. But another door in the kitchen was clearly *not* locked – the fridge door! It sprang open by itself as an avalanche of phantom fruit and veg poured out from inside! Green beans and gooseberries, peppers and pineapples, carrots and kiwi fruits, lentils and

loganberries, radishes and raspberries, out, out, OUT they all tumbled. Soon they turned solid, real and ready to eat, filling the kitchen as Rosa and Marco looked on in dismay.

'Here are your treats,' hissed the vamp-cumber. 'Eat them all up.'

'No way!' said Marco. 'They're . . . fresh.'

'And *good* for us,' Rosa added, her nose screwed up. 'Vile!'

The vamp-cumber smiled. 'You have no choice.'

'We do.' Marco grabbed his bucket of trick-or-treat candy. 'We can eat *this*.'

The vamp-cumber raised a tiny but wicked eyebrow. 'Go ahead and try.'

Greed overcame Marco's fear. He grabbed a chocolate bar from the bucket and tore open the wrapper. Just as he was about to push the sweet treat into his mouth . . .

The were-nana struck! It leaped through the air like a legless, hairy ninja and knocked the choc from Marco's hand.

Rosa grabbed her own chocolate bar. Instantly, the were-nana bounced back and snatched it away.

Marco frowned. 'Your horrible hairy buddy can't keep doing that.'

'That's true, he can't,' said the vamp-cumber with a smile. 'Because . . . I WANT A GO TOO!'

As Marco grabbed for a doughnut, the vamp-cumber shot forwards and bit it with his hideous fangs. In a moment, the doughnut turned green and bumpy – like a cucumber. Marco quickly dropped it. 'Ugh!'

'Next time you reach for something unhealthy, perhaps I'll bite *you*,' the vamp-cumber whispered. 'You'd look much better with green skin and insides full of vitamin K . . .'

Rosa recoiled. 'You wouldn't!'

'I WOULD,' the vamp-cumber chuckled, 'if you and your brother do not change your ways.' The were-nana bounced back beside him, nodding fiercely. 'Between the two of us, we will make sure of it!'

There was a flash of lightning and thunder boomed. Marco and Rosa jumped – and found their creepy visitors had disappeared.

'They've gone,' Marco murmured. 'Maybe we dreamed them?'

Rosa pointed at the fruit and veg all over the kitchen floor. 'This stuff looks real enough – worst luck.' She kicked a turnip – and the were-nana reappeared and nipped her ankle. 'OW!'

'Remember,' came the vamp-cumber's creepy voice from the shadows, 'we will always be watching . . .'

The lights came back on, and Marco and Rosa's mum woke up as if nothing had happened – and soon found her children sitting glumly beside a half-ton of fruit and vegetables.

Marco sighed and looked at her. 'Fancy a snack?'

Ahhhh, poor Marco and Rosa!

They didn't truly believe that the vamp-cumber and the were-nana meant what they said.

Not at first.

Next day, Marco smuggled a sloppy chilli-dog into the toilet with him – but before he could take a bite, the were-nana bounced out of nowhere and knocked it into the toilet bowl.

Rosa took a train out of town for hours, determined to get as far away from home as she could, just to eat a bag of churros. The moment she finally got one out of the bag, the vamp-cumber poofed into sight and chomped the churro first. The doughy sweet snack became a green lump in the blink of an eye. Rosa groaned, and the vamp-cumber chuckled as the girl had to take the train back home with a rumbling stomach.

There was no escape!

It's incredible how much tastier healthy foods become when you have no choice other than to eat them. Rosa and Marco may not *enjoy* a healthier diet, but they put up with it, at least.

See? I told you it was never too late to change.

Sometimes, in the dead of night, they still hear the **THUMP! THUD! THUMP!** of the were-nana on their landing, or spy the vamp-cumber perched on the end of their beds, watching them with gimlet eyes.

If so, they quickly nibble at the emergency salad they keep under their pillows, and hope their supernatural supervisors will leave satisfied. For who wants to feel the

rough fur of a were-nana brush against their cheek? Or the wet rind of a vamp-cumber's tooth scratching at their neck?

Eat well, my sweets! But sweets will always run out in . . .

The End

SPELLS

from MADAME RANA'S SPELL BOOK!

The Charm of Sleeping

It's a good one, this – ideal for enchanting annoying people into
a deep, unstirring sleep! And it's ever so easy to perform.

You will need:

- Tongue of dog (relax, it's just a plant!)
- Calf's snout (relax, it's also just a plant!)
- A chicken (still clucking) (relax, no chickens are harmed
  in the making of this spell!)
- Fifteen poppies, assorted colours (some poppies,
  however, ARE harmed. Get over it.)
- The toenails of a dachshund
- A cauldron fired in the underground
  kitchens of a South Peruvian temple
  (accept no substitutes)

Method:

1) Fill the cauldron with thirty litres of your intended victim's old bathwater.

2) Add the tongue of dog, the calf's snout and then stir in the poppies.

3) Carefully add the chicken and allow it to swim about.

4) Wait until the chicken starts to cluck in soothing tones.

5) Stir five times per minute. (Chew on the dachshund's toenails to aid your concentration.)

6) Fish out the fifteen poppies, squash them into a slimy mess and then leave on the radiator to dry.

7) Empty the cauldron and put the chicken back where you found it.

8) Put the dried poppy mess into a small glass bottle. Ignore for two years.

9) Remember the small glass bottle, whisper:

'Charm of Mandragora

Staying awake's a drag for ya'.

10) Sneak up to your intended victim and make them sniff the bottle.

Ta-daa! Your victim will now sleep very soundly and nothing will wake him or her for ages (as long as you've followed my recipe EXACTLY).

How to Turn Someone into a Toad

As you must know, turning people into toads isn't easy,
so it helps if your target is very toadish to begin with.

You will need:

- A magic wand
- An ivory spoon
- Mud from the bottom of a pond

    (ideally left undisturbed for five years)

- One cupful of the thickest slime you can find
- Seven fresh warts (from a freshwater animal)
- One hundred and sixty-seven empty snail shells
- A worm (for moral support)

Method:

1) Leave your wand in the pond mud for six months.

2) Discuss interesting things with the worm (they're good listeners).

3) Carefully remove the wand and place it point-down in an empty jam jar.

4) Add the slime into the jar with the ivory spoon.

5) Pick a fight with the worm and turn your back on it.

6) Stamp on the snail shells until they are reduced to tiny fragments.

7) Spoon them into the jar around the wand.

8) Make friends with the worm again – life is too short for silly arguments.

9) Add the warts.

10) Go on holiday with the worm for at least three weeks.

11) The day after you return, carefully pull the wand from the jar. DO NOT dislodge any slime, mud or warts still sticking to it.

12) Approach your target with the wand and shout, 'TURN INTO A TOAD!'

13) Wait.

14) If nothing happens, blame the worm and never speak to it again. Then buy a small bottle of Toad Lotion from Hagburn the Vile's Transmogrifcation Parlour on the High Street and slip it into your victim's tea.

Ta-daaaa! It takes a while, but you'll zap them in . . .

The End

Nasty natured Little Toad!

You'd like to hear about another toad? All right, then! I won't beat about the bush. But this latest toad would probably beat UP the bush, the little terror.

Goodness, she's a horrid one. And yet she has such a nice name: Misha Petal.

Doesn't she sound sweet and fragrant?

She's a bright girl. Always done well at school, has friends, keeps her room fairly tidy, all that sort of stuff. You wouldn't think that someone who sounds so nice could be so awful, but Misha has a secret.

You see, Misha Petal HATES the natural world. She hates plants and flowers. She hates animals. She even hates the weather – *any* weather. If she could fall asleep and wake a few hundred years in the future where everyone lives in big plastic bubbles and beams from one spot to another without having to go outside at all, she would be very, very happy, thank you very much.

There is no love of nature in Misha's nature.

For instance, most people are sad that the world's rainforests are disappearing.

Not Misha.

While thousands sign petitions to save the rainforests, Misha did not.

'Who wants a forest where it's raining all the time?' was Misha's wonky logic. 'It must be so wet, you can't even turn it into firewood! Just blow up the stupid rainforests so we can get on with our lives.'

If you overheard someone being this ignorant, you might be tempted to say, 'What about all the millions of animals who live in rainforests? They need to be saved.' You would be caring and sensible if you did.

Misha Petal, however, would not agree.

'Scientists are always moaning about wild animals going extinct,' she'd say. 'The sooner ALL the animals are extinct, the sooner we'll stop being bored to death.'

It's a harsh and misguided view, I agree. But that was what Misha believed.

When beautiful countryside is threatened by new roads or new houses, many people rush to protect and preserve it.

Not Misha.

Misha spends hours on the phone each week trying to persuade builders to move in and demolish every green space for miles around her house.

'What's wrong with you?' she cries. 'Who cares if that woodland has a preservation order on it? Pretend you got the wrong address and crush it into matchsticks!'

You might be wondering why Misha is so unnaturally anti-natural.

Well, it all begins with her parents. They love the outdoors life, and from an early age, Misha was taken on camping trips and nature hikes and pony treks and mountain climbs and so on.

She hated every single one of them.

Every Sunday they would drag her on a walk around the local beauty spots.

'It's soooooooooooo boring!' Misha moaned. 'I want to stay home and play on the computer.'

'Well, you can't,' said her dad briskly.

Misha always brought her phone on the walk so she had something to look at besides – ugh – *nature*. She spent every step staring at her screen, messaging her friends or playing apps. She plugged in her headphones as well so the beat of her music drowned out the irritating sound of birdsong, gurgling brooks and humming bumblebees.

However, there came a day when Misha's mum put a stop to this.

'You spend enough time on your phone,' she said firmly. 'Just for an hour, Misha, leave it at home and look at the world about you. See the flowers. Hear the birds and insects. Look at the patterns the sunlight makes on the stream.'

'I've seen better patterns on a pair of old pants!' Misha grumbled.

Her parents refused to cave in to her tears or her temper and as a result, Misha had to actually look around her on the walk. She did not like what she saw. Long green grass, beautiful flowers, pretty hedgerows – oh, such hideous natural things, all about her!

While her mum and dad walked hand-in-hand in wonder, a sly smile took root on Misha's face. *If Mum and Dad are so keen for me to walk*, she thought, *then I shall walk – all over their precious flowers*!

Targeting a patch of bluebells (not that she had the remotest idea *what* they were called) she trampled them, till they were squashed flat. Then she pulled some sweet wrappers from her pocket and dropped them in the mud.

'Are you all right, Misha?' her mum called.

'Just giving some flowers my attention,' Misha called back, grinding the last one under her heel.

How glorious it was to destroy in moments what nature had taken so long to grow! On that first walk alone she kicked the heads off daffodils, crushed blooms and bounced on a baby blackberry bush.

That last encounter taught her that, sometimes, nature fights back with some well-placed thorns.

Did that put Misha off?

Not at all.

It made her swear a vile revenge, not just against blackberries but against all plants.

The following Sunday, Misha once again found there was no escaping a walk – and so she decided to make the most of it.

'Can I borrow your spare wellies, Mum?' she asked craftily.

'Of course!' Mum beamed. 'You can make them as mucky as you like.'

Mucky with FLOWER BLOOD and LITTER, thought Misha. She stuffed her pockets with rubbish and then, whenever her parents weren't looking, she got busy picking petunias, punching sunflowers and murdering marigolds in their beds. After committing this floral mayhem she left behind a trail of empty crisp packets, chewed gum and squashed juice boxes as she walked, like an awful one-girl Hansel and Gretel.

The Countryside Code says we should respect, protect and enjoy the outdoors. But Misha did her best to spoil it whenever she could. It wasn't only wild plants she targeted, but those in the gardens they passed on the way to the woods. Misha decided that she particularly hated roses,

with their large, romantic blooms
and fierce thorns. Rose bushes
were difficult to stamp on, so as
she passed them she settled for
snipping off as many buds and
flowers as she could with her
dad's garden shears before anyone
noticed what she was up to. (Her record, should you be
interested, was eighteen roses in seven seconds.)

All the time, her parents thought they had changed
their daughter's mind about the 'horrors' of nature, and that
she looked forward to their walks. If only they'd caught
her in the act of bumping off the bougainvillea or dumping
rubbish on the rhododendrons! But they did not.

*

One day her dad asked her, 'Do you want the good news or
the bad news?'

Misha considered. The 'good' news was probably some
dumb story about elephant poachers being locked up (Misha
would've given them a medal instead!), and the 'bad' news
that some rare species of miniature monkey had died out
(Misha would've danced on its tiny grave if she could!).

'Give me the bad news,' she sighed at last.

'The bad news,' said Dad, 'is that we're not going for a
walk on Sunday.'

'Oh, dear,' Misha snorted, although it *was* bad news in some ways – her pockets were stuffed with some very loathsome litter she'd been planning to scatter through the woods! 'What's the good news?'

'The good news is that the reason we're not going for a walk is because we'll be heading to the park for the town's thousandth anniversary celebrations!' Dad grinned. 'Don't you remember us telling you? Volunteers have planted a thousand different coloured flowers to make a giant display of the town's coat of arms. Two stags, a ship, the ocean, a crown, a swan . . .'

'It looks incredible!' Mum came bustling up. 'Your dad and I helped. It took us days and days. It's going to be unveiled by the mayor in front of the whole town.'

'Well,' said Misha, 'that *is* good news.' *But bad news for the town*, she thought privately, for she had suddenly been struck by a very wicked idea.

An idea that was so exciting, some might lose their heads over it . . .

✳

Well past her bedtime on Saturday night, Misha sneaked out of the house with her dad's garden shears and hurried to the park.

The gates were locked, she discovered; but railings weren't going to stop her now!

Misha chose a quiet spot and climbed over. Then, in the silvery moonlight, she looked for the great flower display, kicking saplings as she went.

It didn't take her long to find the floral coat of arms, hidden beneath a vast, white plastic sheet, ready for the big reveal. Misha chuckled as she unpegged the plastic sheet

and pulled it back. Even in the dark, it was an impressive sight – each flower of each colour in just the right place.

But not for much longer!

Misha's rose-rage had given her a taste for cutting off flower heads.

Now, she would snip the bloom from EVERY SINGLE FLOWER IN THE DISPLAY!

All one thousand of them!

'Coat of arms? Ha!' Misha sniggered. 'Prepare to be turned into a vest of broken fingers . . . !'

SNIP! The first flower to fall was a red zinnia. Misha squashed it in her fist, threw it over her shoulder, and then snipped the bloom beside it . . . and the next . . . and the next . . .

Before she knew it, she was hacking away at the floral display like a weapons-grade anti-gardener. Oh, what a toxic toad!

Petals flew all around as Ms Petal flew all around, decapitating the poor plants in their neat little rows, chopping and hacking and snipping and snapping until in the end . . .

Not a solitary flower still stood.

Dizzy with delight, her fingers sticky with spilled plant sap, Misha pulled back the plastic sheet and pegged it down. How the town would gasp tomorrow when her handiwork was revealed! How the volunteers would groan and the old people cry and the mayor faint and . . .

For a moment in the moonlight, deep inside, Misha felt an unexpected stab of guilt.

Perhaps she had gone too far?

Then a cold wind blew up out of nowhere and rustled the headless stalks. It was an eerie, bone-chilling sound and it seemed to whisper to Misha: *You'll be sorry . . .*

With a shiver, Misha raced across the park, scrambled over the gates and ran home.

It was a long, scary journey. The moon no longer shone, buried by muddy clouds, and the streetlamps had gone out. The bushes and grasses in the night gardens rustled furiously as she passed – even though the wind had dropped . . .

It's just my imagination, thought Misha anxiously. *That's all!*

But, as you must surely know . . . it was not.

By the time Misha had crept back inside the house and tiptoed to bed, she was sweaty and scared and shaking. The image of the flower stalks bending in the supernatural wind haunted her each time she closed her eyes. She turned on the torch in her phone to give some comforting light . . . but it went dead in seconds, even though she'd charged it that very night.

Misha tried to calm her breathing. *Just close your eyes and go to sleep*, she told herself.

No sooner had her eyes closed than there was a tap-tap-tapping at the window.

'Wha—?' Misha sat up in bed. Branches were brushing at her window, twigs pushing towards the bottom of the frame.

And yet, NO TREE GREW OUTSIDE HER WINDOW.

Misha wanted to scream, but the noise died in her throat. Had the thousand flowers screamed silently as she'd slit their stems? She sat, spellbound in horror, as the window was forced open by the questing, quivering tree branches . . .

Finally, she broke the spell, jumped out of bed and threw open her bedroom door.

Two gigantic Venus flytraps loomed there, creeping forwards on soil-shaking roots, their stalks a-tremble and planty jaws gnashing.

Misha knew why they were
here – and what they wanted.
'No, please! I'm sorry I
lopped off the flowers'
heads. Don't do the same
to me! Don't!'

The mahoosive
monster plants ignored
her, swishing inside
the bedroom, bitey
leaves jostling, buds
breakdancing on their
twisty, turning bodies.
Misha backed away – straight into the tree. She felt the
twitching tendrils coil around her ankles and shrieked as
she was tugged into the air. Was that a face in the bark,
leering at her from the tree-trunk . . . ?

Misha turned to find fresh terror waiting for her. Blades
of grass were growing on the bedroom carpet. And these
really were blades, let me tell you! Each as sharp as a knife,
stretching taller all the time as if straining to reach her. If the
tree's tangled branches dropped her now—

Even as she thought it, that's what happened!

Before she could try to scream again, the Venus flytraps
caught her in their fearsome grip. The sticky jaws of their
leaves closed around her limbs – closed and *tightened*. The

branches about her clapped as an icy wind blew through the window, rustling the blades of grass as they grew ever longer. She tried to pull her head away but the grassy spikes were getting closer and closer.

A brilliant light that came from nowhere dazzled her.

Misha woke up.

She screamed.

Because an enormous lorry had lost control, swerved off the road and was now heading straight for her bedroom window!

KERBOOM!

The noise was a lot worse than that, but you'll have to take my word for it. When speeding truck meets bungalow, it rarely ends well.

And would you believe what this lorry was carrying?

It happened to be the lorry that collects garden waste from those big wheelie-bins at the side of the road.

All the grass clippings and hedge trimmings and seed cases and dead leaves and mulch from across town – you could call it Nature's Litter, couldn't you? – well, that night, it burst out of the overturned lorry and came crashing through Misha's bedroom window.

She, along with everything she owned, was buried in a dark green avalanche.

It was rather poetic, really. After all, Misha had been using the outdoors as her own rubbish bin for quite some

time. It was perhaps only right that the outdoors got to use her bedroom in the same way.

'Get me out!' Misha screamed. 'I'm sorry I chopped the flowers' heads off! I'm sorry I ruined the display! Don't take *my* head off, please!'

Appalled by their daughter's shocking confession as they were, Mr and Mrs Petal still had to dig her out, of course. They were glad to find she hadn't been harmed.

Well, not by the lorry crash, at least.

She'd tried so hard to keep her head in the midst of her terrifying dream that when the crashing lorry scared her awake it had had a most curious effect.

Misha's head had shrunk back into her body! In place of a face, all you could see was a pair of eyes peeping out from her shoulders, beneath her mop of hair.

It wasn't a very good look, I have to say.

Still, at least it made it easier for her to avoid the accusing stares of the townspeople when her parents made her confess to what she'd done to their great flower display.

Happily, some good did come from this toad's diabolical handiwork. The townspeople were so shocked by Misha's great flower massacre that they pulled together and got planting all over again.

It wasn't quite so tidy, and the colours didn't match, and it was very late in the evening when the design was completed, but the town was able to celebrate its impressive

anniversary – and it did so as a closer community than ever before.

Misha is not a welcome part of that community, but she *has* finally done something to help the natural world. Her head can still shrink back into her body to this day; however hard she tries she can't push it right back out again. She looks a lot like a tortoise – and, did you know, over half of all the species of tortoise and turtles alive today are close to extinction? So, much to Misha's disgust, her parents now send her all over the world to help raise awareness for these vulnerable creatures.

It reminds her that certain types of *toad* could turn out to be an endangered species in . . .

The End

Lying Little Toad!

Have you ever done something quite impressive and wanted to share the news with everyone you meet? Have you ever been so pleased with yourself you couldn't stop talking about it?

And if you have, did someone accuse you of showing off? Or say, 'Shut up, no way, you're making things up'?

If they did, you were probably a bit miffed. I expect you didn't mean to show off, you were just excited. You should have heard me when I found out that this book was going to be published! I was twittering about it all over antisocial media (it's how we modern witches communicate – like your social media, but with more curses and spells), posting the cover on Broomstagram and Twitcher and some online trolls told me that *I* was showing off (and on antisocial media they're REAL trolls, so you don't want to mess with them).

Anyway, what I'm trying to say is, everyone shows off sometimes – but if you're the sort who shows off *all* the time, chances are you'll annoy everyone around you. What's worse is if you've never done anything impressive in your life and you *make up things* to boast about . . .  like a lying little toad I know called Gustav Munch.

He might've been short, but Gustav was a master of tall tales.

I'm not talking little white lies like, 'Yes, of course I cleaned my teeth this morning!'

I'm talking dirty big fat whoppers like, 'At school there was a competition to find out who was the best child ever in the world, and I didn't even enter it but somehow I still came first and won it because all the teachers think I'm *that* brilliant!'

Yes, that lie was actually told by Gustav to his mum, who still believes it to this day.

Sadly, Gustav is not the best child ever in the world. He is a lazy boy who lies because it's less effort than doing things for real.

Just the other day, after school, Gustav was smirking at his classmates as they practised a dance routine in the park for a competition. He certainly couldn't be bothered to help them out! Patsy, who lived next door to Gustav, was watching with her mum, and asked why Gustav didn't join in. Gustav, as ever, decided to make something up.

'I'm not allowed to,' he explained. 'I'm so incredibly good at dancing, the professional dance leagues have banned me from taking part at an amateur level.'

'No way!' Patsy gasped. She was an innocent child and believed him. 'Well, do you want to play catch with me?'

'I'm not allowed to play catch either. I'm too good.' Gustav yawned. 'NASA have banned me.'

'NASA? You mean, the space agency? Why would they ban you?'

'They can't risk me hurting my hands,' Gustav revealed. 'They have me on speed-dial – if a meteorite is about to smash down on the town, they need me to catch it before it hits.'

Patsy's eyes widened. 'Wow! Really?'

'I'm the Planet Earth's last line of defence.' Gustav nodded. 'I'm just basically awesome.'

'Cool!' Patsy grinned. 'Wait till I tell my friends . . .'

'I, er, wouldn't do that,' said Gustav quickly, 'because actually . . . you don't have any friends.' He chuckled. 'They told me earlier that they think you smell and that they hate you.'

'No!' Patsy's face fell. 'You . . . you're making it up!'

'Nope!' Gustav shook his head. 'Cross my heart and hope to die.'

As Patsy ran off with tears in her eyes, Gustav smiled nastily and hurried into the nearby trees. 'Another one tricked!'

'Excuse me,' came a quiet voice from somewhere behind him. 'Is that girl upset? Did you say, "another one tricked"?'

'What? Er, no!' Gustav swiftly snatched up a twig from the ground. 'I said, "Another *fun stick*"! I love playing outside, isn't exercise the best?'

'Mm-hmm.' In front of Gustav stood a thin, weaselly

boy with red cheeks, keen eyes and a mess of dark hair. But what Gustav noticed straightaway was that the boy was wearing a pair of bright satin shorts over his trousers: they were red with orange flames embroidered up the sides, and they were spotlessly clean, even though the trousers beneath were filthy and ragged.

Without knowing quite why, Gustav longed to wear those red shorts himself, all the time – they were the snazziest shorts he'd ever seen!

'How do you do?' said Gustav. 'I'm Gustav Munch. I'm . . . I'm the son of a fashion designer.'

This was, as you have guessed, of course, a total lie. Gustav's dad worked in the sewers.

The boy nodded. 'Hello, Gustav Munch! I've heard of you. I'm Owen Bowen. What do you think of my special designer pants?'

'Those shorts you're wearing over your trousers, you mean?' Gustav didn't want Owen Bowen to know how much he wanted them for himself. 'I can't tell a lie, Owen: they're awful. Ugh! You look like Superman gone wrong!'

'Really?' The boy raised his patchy eyebrows. 'Oh, dear.'

Gustav nodded. 'You know Patsy – that girl who ran away just now? She was actually running from your shorts! She's going to fetch the police to arrest you for crimes against leg-based fashion! So if you don't want to go to prison, you should chuck those shorts away. Sling them in the bin, and fast!'

The boy shook his head. 'I can't do that. But I could *give* them to somebody . . . somebody who'd wear them in my place.'

'Oh, yes?' Gustav couldn't believe his luck. He tried to play things cool and immediately lied again. 'Well . . . I'm, er, having a fancy dress party where everyone has to wear the worst clothes they can find. Those shorts *might* do for my costume . . .'

'In that case, I'm sure you'd like to know if they fit.' Owen Bowen's eyes glittered. 'You must try them on.'

Gustav pretended to yawn. 'Go on, then.'

In a second, Owen Bowen had whipped off his red shorts and flipped them into Gustav's face. 'YESSSSSSSSSSSSS! There you are. They're all yours! YOURS TO KEEP! Ha, ha, ha!'

What a weirdo, thought Gustav, as he pulled on the shorts over his jeans. They were a bit baggy . . . but not for long! Within a few moments, they shrank to fit him perfectly. 'Hey, what's going on?'

'I'm FREE, that's what!' Owen did a (rather peculiar) dance for joy. 'Now YOU are the prisoner of the pants.'

'The *what* now?' Gustav spluttered.

'Allow me to show you.' Owen chuckled. 'So, you're really the son of a fashion designer?'

'Um, yes, of course I am,' Gustav said. But as he spoke he felt a wave of great heat in his bottom area. Suddenly the embroidered flames on the shorts glowed red hot! '*ARRRRGH*!' Gustav cried.

'Liar, liar, pants on fire!' Owen bellowed. 'That's what's going to happen to you every time you tell a lie.'

'I don't believe you,' said Gustav – and howled again as the shorts burned his butt. 'Oh. I guess I *do* believe you.'

'You ought to. I'm telling the truth – for once. You see, I used to be a brilliant liar, until I met a girl wearing those magic pants and she tricked *me* into wearing them.' He shrugged. 'That was it: I couldn't tell a lie ever again, unless I wanted a toasted bum. Magical fiery pants certainly take the fun out of lying, just you wait and see!'

'But what about when I take a bath or put on my pyjamas at night?' said Gustav.

'You can pull the shorts down but they'll never come off,' said Owen. 'Not until you choose in your heart never to lie again – or until you find a liar as awful as you are and pass on the pants to them. And I think you'll find that tricky. I've been hunting for months, and I'm not sure there's ANY liar as bad as you.' Owen walked away, waving cheerfully. 'Thanks for setting me free, fool! Bye!'

'No!' wailed Gustav. 'You can't leave me like this!'

Owen paused. 'You're right. I can't.' Then he laughed. 'Ha! That was a lie – I totally can leave you. Yay, I can lie again! *Bye*, again!' And with that, still hooting with wicked mirth, Owen Bowen was gone.

Gustav walked home in a daze, frowning down at the red pants. 'It must have been miserable *magic* that made me want them,' he muttered. 'What am I going to do now?'

'Oooh, those are nice shorts,' said his mum as he came in. 'Where did you get them?'

Without thinking, Gustav lied. 'I bought them from a charity shop— *YIIIEEEEEEEEE*!' The pants grew red hot and Gustav jumped so high in the air he banged his head on the ceiling. '*OWWW*! I mean, a nun was selling clothes to raise money for the poor and— *YIEEEEEEEEEEEEEE*!' Gustav wiggled like a worm in a frying pan as his rump got grilled. 'I mean, I found them in the *WOOOOOOOOOOOOOOOOOODS*!' His buttocks blazed, and Gustav had to jump into the kitchen sink and turn on the taps to stop the burning.

Gustav's mum stared at him. 'Whatever are you doing in the sink, Gustav?'

'Shut up!' Gustav groaned. 'I've got to figure out a way to get these pants off!'

He rushed to the bathroom, locked the door and pulled them down. But they stuck to his ankles and refused to budge.

He tried to cut them with his mum's dressmaking scissors, but the scissor blades drooped like rubber every time they touched the fabric.

He ran to the garage to fetch his dad's crowbar and tried to prise off the pants. 'Nnnnnnnnnng,' he heaved. 'Rrrrrrrrrrrghhhhhhh . . .'

'What are you up to?' his mum called warily from the house.

'Nothing,' Gustav gasped – and then shrieked as the liar-liar pants went on fire again. 'My lower cheeks will be charred for ever if I can't do something!'

Of course, there was something he could've done. He could've decided to stop his constant lying. Then the liar-liar pants would've remained merely an unusual fashion statement and eventually fallen off all by themselves. But the idea of not lying was as crazy to Gustav as the idea of not breathing. The foolish little toad simply could not do it.

For the rest of the afternoon he ran about trying to get himself out of the sinister shorts.

Gustav went back to the park and tried to catapult himself out of them using two trees, a fishing line and a length of elastic.

It didn't work. Gustav knew he would have to be more ingenious.

He tried pulling his shorts down around his ankles and staking them to the ground while holding a large plastic sheet above his head. 'Now, if I lie really badly, the burning effect will create hot air. The hot air will fill the sheet just like a hot air balloon and lift me into the sky – while the liar-liar pants stay pinned to the ground!' Bracing himself, he took a deep breath and announced: 'I am the king of Belgium! **OW**!' His posterior pulsed harder with heat with every lie he told. 'My house is the Taj Mahal! **OWW-OOOO**! I once ate seventy-two burgers in one night – **AAAGH** . . . !' The shorts might have been around his ankles but Gustav's butt was still ablaze. The air about him grew hotter . . . and hotter . . . the plastic sheet swelled and Gustav began to rise into the air . . . !

Then the plastic shrivelled and melted and Gustav dropped back to earth on his half-roasted bottom. The shorts quivered, almost as if they were laughing.

There must be a way to beat them, thought Gustav, yanking them up again. He ran through the park, racking his brains. As he passed his classmates who were still practising their dance routine, he almost crashed into Patsy from next door.

'You!' Patsy scowled at him. 'You're a big fat liar.'

'No, I'm not,' said Gustav – but his high-temperature tail-end told a different story. '**OW**!'

'You are!' Patsy insisted. 'My mum talked to my friends. They never said anything nasty about me.'

Gustav snorted. He was proud of his lies and didn't want her seeing through them so quickly. 'Duh! They wouldn't tell your mum the truth, would they?' he said. 'I heard them just now saying how much they hated you—*OOOOOOOOOOO*!' His bottom burned so badly his eyes watered.

If I want to keep lying I have to learn to bear the pain, thought Gustav grimly. *I can't give in. I won't!*

'I don't believe you,' Patsy said. 'I don't believe you're a brilliant dancer either.'

'I am!' Gustav said. '**OWWWW**!!!'

'You're not,' said Patsy. 'I checked with your classmates. They've never seen you dance a step.'

'I told you, I'm banned for being too good.' Gustav gritted his teeth. '**ARRRRRRGH**!'

'You would still dance just for fun,' said Patsy, 'if you were really a brilliant dancer.'

'I AM a brilliant dancer . . .' Gustav trailed off as his rear began to sizzle. He hopped up and down and jumped and twirled about, trying to contain the pain. 'Argh . . . I've won fifty dancing awards! I arrange all the routines on TV dance shows! I am the reigning regional cha-cha-cha champion!' *It doesn't hurt, it doesn't hurt, it doesn't hurt . . .*

Oh, but it did! The burn in his buns was growing unbearable.

'**OWWWWW**!' Gustav twittered on tippy-toes, contorted and crawled, spun on the spot and leaped like a toad on a hotplate, but still he went on lying. 'I am a FANTASTIC dancer. I am a SUPER-SUPERB dancer . . . !' The bottom barbecue grew worse with every fib, but Gustav kept going, shimmying and shuddering, high kicking and handstanding, bumping and bending and backflipping . . . until, finally, he fell over backwards and lay, panting for breath.

His class stared in awe and wonder. 'Well, how about that,' a boy said. 'He really IS an amazing dancer!'

Huh? thought Gustav, still fighting for breath.

'That is the most incredible dance routine I've ever seen,' a girl added.

Gustav hardly heard her. All he knew was – the shorts had stopped burning. He pulled them down and they did not fry his fingers. Cautiously, he hooked them over his shoes. Off they came.

Slowly, understanding began to dawn. 'Of course,' he breathed. 'I lied when I said I was a fantastic dancer so the liar-liar pants burned – but the burning turned me INTO a fantastic dancer. The lie became the truth and the shorts couldn't handle it!' He looked down, and with a flood of relief saw the pants wriggling away into the woods at high speed. 'Ha! In your face, pants!'

'So you *were* telling the truth,' said Patsy sadly. 'I suppose that what you said about my friends hating me was true too, then.'

'Yes, it was!' roared Gustav. He had seen off the shorts and could lie all he liked! 'Totally, grade-A true.'

Patsy had stopped looking at him; now she was staring up at the sky. 'And it was true when you said that if

a meteorite is about to
smash down on the town,
you're the one who's meant to
catch it?'

'Totally true,' Gustav agreed with a smirk.

But what was that strange whistling sound coming out of the sky? Why was it getting dark? Why was Patsy suddenly running away like crazy, together with everyone else in the park?

Gustav looked up and saw the meteorite shooting through the sky straight towards him. Do you think, just before it hit, he guessed the real reason the shorts took off like they did?

Call me a silly old witch, but I like to think he did.

BOOOM!

When he gets out of the hospital, I must remember to ask him! I'm sure he'll be quite glad to have the rest of his body hurting for a change, instead of that burning sensation in . . .

The End

WITCHES' BREW

Witches like me use all kinds of ingredients in the spells
we weave. To stop ordinary people from trying to copy our
spells, we often use old, unusual names for the ingredients.
Look at the following famous witchy ingredients –
can you tell what they really are?

1. 'Eye of Newt' is actually:

a) the eye of a newt

b) a mustard seed

c) the centre of a white flower such as a daisy

2. 'Wool of bat' is actually:

a) holly leaves

b) skin taken from a bat

c) wood shavings from a sports bat

3. 'Adder's fork' is actually:

a) cress

b) the tongue of an adder

c) a way of combining ingredients

4. 'Toe of frog' is actually:

    a) a daisy

    b) toadflax, a type of plant

    c) a buttercup

5. 'Blindworm' is actually:

    a) a slow worm

    b) a headless worm

    c) a tailless worm

6. 'Tongue of dog' is actually:

    a) the tongue of a dog

    b) a long, thin sausage

    c) houndstongue, a plant with rough leaves

7. 'Cat's foot' is actually:

    a) a type of Indian tea

    b) ivy

    c) the foot of a cat

8. 'Bird's foot' is actually:

    a) the foot of a bird

    b) moss

    c) fenugreek, a herb

Answers: 1. b; 2. a; 3. b; 4. c; 5. a; 6. c; 7. b; 8. c.

Pop Goes the Little Toad!

I've just had a cup of tea. How's THAT for an exciting opening, eh? Well, it's true, and I only mention it because I'm rather afraid my cat might have *done* something in my cup before I poured the tea. You see, it tasted oddly fizzy . . . and I'm not very fond of fizzy drinks.

Are you?

I know a lot of children who enjoy lemonade and orangeade and cola and cream soda and all sorts of sugary delights. However, these drinks can be bad for your health.

Very, very bad.

For some children, a sticky, fizzy drink is a treat they have now and then. For others, it is something they chug back all the time, and they really shouldn't.

They really, *really* shouldn't.

Yes, I'm speaking from experience and, no, it will come as no surprise to you by now that I know a toad who is EXTREMELY fond of fizzy drinks. She lives by the seaside in what might be a house – it's hard to tell from the way the empty drink cans have filled the garden and piled up around the building itself.

This is Anya Gopopov. She'd wave at you, but doesn't want to spill a drop of her favourite pop. And in case you're wondering, her favourite pop is ALL of them – and usually all at once. You can tell by counting the different coloured cans, next time you have a spare couple of weeks.

Of course, gulping down the bubbles as she does, Anya Gopopov has a lot of trapped wind. In fact, she belches more than she speaks, and she's learned to communicate almost entirely through hiccups and burps.

'*Rrrrrp-GuRRRRRRRRRRRR!*' for instance, means, 'I need more cans of pop, NOW.'

'*BRRRRRRPH-veeeeeee!*' (a sound that makes her pigtails stand on end) means, 'GANGWAY, I'm busting for a wee.'

'*BRuRRRRRRRRRP-hrrrrrrrrrrr!*' means, 'Give me your money, I'm going down the shops to buy some more cans of pop because we've run out of them for the second time TODAY.'

And '*Prhprhphrrr-aaaar!*' means, 'Ha, ha, I chucked away an empty can and hit a seagull on the head.' (Anya Gopopov hates seagulls and has toadishly bombarded them ever since one accidentally knocked over a full can of cola at the beach; sadly she now considers turning cans into anti-seagull missiles a form of recycling.)

Nasty little Anya Gopopov, waddling and burping along the street, all that festering syrup swilling about inside her like brine in a barrel, flinging her empty cans at every seagull. What a poor diet and poorer life she has! Although it's her *mum* who's really poor, since almost everything she earns is spent by Anya Gopopov on her sparkling habit.

How did this toad come to have such a thirst for fizz? I'm afraid her mum has to take some of the blame. She is an absent-minded woman and, when Anya Gopopov was small, used to mix up her own cherry cola with her baby's milk. So Anya Gopopov was fizzing from her earliest days, and it did her no favours (whereas all that milk has left her mum's bones in wonderful shape).

You see, there's nothing very good in fizzy drinks – just flavourings and big spoonfuls of sugar or sweeteners. But when it comes to fizzy drinks, Anya Gopopov believes that you can *never* have too much.

Or, at least, she used to believe that.

Alas, things changed dramatically for Anya Gopopov with a terrible swiftness. The same swiftness with which a gull can flap its wings.

She had just come out of the supermarket with a shopping trolley PILED HIGH with cola cans on special offer. There must have been three hundred in there, for the same price as one hundred and fifty! Anya Gopopov was so happy she performed her favourite dance (the can-can, of course) and started tucking into her fizzy feast there and then in the supermarket car park.

A seagull landed nearby and eyed her beadily.

'**BRR-URRRRRRP!**' Anya Gopopov belched in its direction, an action that has been known to stun a smaller bird.

The gull ignored her and went on staring.

Enraged, Anya Gopopov drained her can and threw it at the gull. The gull simply sidestepped out of its way with surprising dignity for a shameless, squawky chip-stealer.

Anya Gopopov was not to be defeated. **GULP-GULP-GULP!** Another can-full of cola rocketed down her gullet. She tossed the empty can into the air and jerked her head so that her pigtail struck it like a hairy bat. **CLANG!** The can flew at its feathered target with uncanny precision, but the seagull hopped aside once more and gave a mocking '**CARRRR!**'

Anya Gopopov downed another can and tried again. '**Prhprhphrrr-aaaar!**'

'**CA-CARRR!**' the gull retorted, jumping over the clumsy missile. Then it turned and walked away.

'No, you **BRR-vrr-RRRRRRRP**,' Anya Gopopov whispered and rumbled at the gull's tail feathers. She was filled with a roaring rage and an awful lot of cola – and that quantity was about to become more awful still. She staggered after the gull, glugging down *eight* cans, one after the other, and hurled each one of them rapid-fire at the annoying bird.

The gull avoided each can without effort.

'**URRRRRP**!' Anya Gopopov cracked open another six-pack. She was feeling decidedly **BRRRRRRPH-veeeeeee**! – but she couldn't break off for a wee now, and let the gull get away. She had to make it pay for its challenge! No stupid seagull was going to outwit her.

Of course, the seagull was not stupid. Perhaps it was a special bird – a hired expert wing-man drafted in by some of the many gulls around town with bumps on their heads, to teach Anya Gopopov a lesson. Perhaps it was some crafty shape-shifting witch, up to tricks in the guise of a bird? We may never know for sure.

But Anya Gopopov was about to learn that being unkind to animals NEVER ends well.

She kept drinking the fizz and thwacking the cans – **GLUG! CLANG! CARR! GLUG! KLONK! CA-CARRRR!** And the fizz did its biz. The bubbles inside her couldn't escape fast enough.

As she drank and drank and drank, Anya Gopopov began to inflate.

Her dress started to stretch. Her cardigan rose over her bulging belly. The gull gave a creaking cry that might have been laughter, and launched into the blue sky.

Slowly, Anya Gopopov floated into the air after it.

'How frightening!' I hear you cry. (If not you, then someone else nearby, I'm sure.)

But Anya Gopopov did not think her predicament was frightening at all. By now, she had more fizzy drinks in her belly than a newly fuelled tanker full of petrol. The shock of so many additives hitting her system at once was bamboozling her brain.

I love bubbles so much, she thought, *and now I've BECOME ONE!*

Her pigtails were flapping about like ratty rotor blades. *Ha, ha! I'm flying!* she thought. *There is NOWHERE this grotty gull can hide from me!*

(At least, she *probably* thought that; it came out as, '**Rrrr-brrrrr-UPHHHHHHG!**' so it's hard to tell for sure.)

Up Anya Gopopov floated, high into the air, clutching cans to her inflated tum, drinking and rising ever higher. The gull flapped lazily around her as if daring her to drink more and test her aim – a challenge Anya Gopopov was all too willing to take.

'**BRRRRP.**' **WHEEE!** The empty cans tumbled through the air, missed the gull and fell to earth far below. **CLANG! KRUNK! SPLOOSH!**

SPLOOSH? Anya Gopopov frowned. *What made the sploosh?* She was the size of a hot-air balloon by now, spinning about, but as she glanced down with some difficulty she saw she'd drifted over a large reservoir, where the town's drinking water came from.

Oooh, thought Anya Gopopov. *This would be a good place to wee! I really am busting . . .*

But before she could release her homemade lemonade, the gull decided it had lulled Anya Gopopov into a false sense of security for long enough.

Now was the time to strike – and strike it did!

'*CA-CARRRRRRRR!*' The seagull flapped right up to the fully inflated Anya Gopopov and pecked her with all the force its feathered form could muster.

You can guess what happened next:

POP!

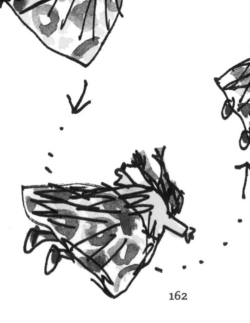

With a loud belching noise and a high-pitched farty whine, Anya Gopopov went spinning out of control, streaking

through the skies like a pig-tailed comet. She flew the way
bricks do and splashed down into the water . . .

Pure, unbubbled, untroubled water.

Plain, refreshing, clear water.

Water – that natural elixir without which no animal
can survive!

Of course, Anya Gopopov couldn't help but swallow a
couple of gulps.

Oh, dear.

The shock of its plain liquid perfection made her hair fall out! Down it dropped in a tangled avalanche, and – *splish*, *splash*, *splosh* – I'm afraid that her rotten teeth were not far behind.

'*VrrrrrRRRP!*' she burped in horror, gnashing her gums as more gulls swooped to collect her fallen hair.

(Don't worry – those birds took each and every strand and wove fabulous nests with the stuff, so it didn't go to waste.)

As for Anya Gopopov, she stayed splashing about for half an hour before she was picked up by a fishing boat. The crew nearly threw her straight back in, but in the end they hauled her to shore. What a sorry sight she looked, hairless and toothless, her stretched-out skin sagging about her and her gums chattering with the cold.

Anya Gopopov tried to find her abandoned trolley full of fizz, but it had been taken away. Her mum was FURIOUS with her for wasting so much money and bringing home nothing to show for it; she declared that from now on they would have nothing to drink but tap water.

Of course, Anya Gopopov wailed and burped so loudly and angrily that she was sent straight to her bedroom. She

flopped furiously on the bed, where she
was taunted by the rude laughter of the
wheeling seagulls outside – one of whom
was wearing an extraordinary toupee
that might just have been made from a
toady girl's missing pigtail . . .

You see? I told you, didn't I? Fizzy drinks really are bad
for your health.

Gullty as charged! Ha, ha, ha, I hope that bad puns
don't drive you round . . .

The (B)end

Square-eyed Little Toad!

I know, I know. You probably have me down as an old fuddy-duddy whose idea of a mobile phone is a big red telephone box on wheels.

You little cheeker!

If you *do* think that, you are wrong! We witches have to move with the times. I mean, I *could* contact my witchy friends by casting a spell of ectoplasmic transference and whooshing about the world in my intangible astral form but – oh! – it plays havoc with my tummy and once I'm done I'm stuck on the loo for hours after. It's much easier to send a text.

I don't have an iPad but I have something that's even better – an *L*-Pad! That's a *Lily* Pad, of course. I use it to keep frogs on. Very useful things for spells, frogs, almost as useful as TOADS. All of which reminds me of a young toad of my acquaintance who was, shall we say, over-fond of technology – and in particular, screen games . . .

Ah, yes, young Song Jinwoo . . . he was always glued to his gadgets. His mum and dad worked for a big video games developer and, from his earliest days, Song got to try them out. Mr and Mrs Jinwoo never had any trouble getting him off to sleep as an infant – because they didn't even try. Song would just lie there in his cot, his little baby fingers and thumbs wrapped around a controller, staring at a seventy-two inch screen on the wall as he ran through battlefields, raced in cars and spaceships, blew up monsters and all sorts!

Most people's first words are things like, 'Mama!' or 'car' or something simple like that. Song's first words were, 'Central Processing Unit'. How his parents sighed with delight – until Song quickly followed those words by screaming, 'GIMME BETTER FASTER ONE!' at ear-splitting volume.

As he grew bigger, so did Song's appetite for games. He was a natural pro player, and from the age of two became much in demand as a product-tester. This meant that he found himself constantly showered with consoles, handhelds and brand-new games, often testing them before they reached the shops.

You might be thinking, *Lucky young Song*! However, I'm afraid that Song did not appreciate his good fortune. He never said thank you. He rarely said anything at all – apart from, 'NOT FAIR!', 'THIS STINKS!' or 'NOOOOOO, THE GAME GLITCHED OUT, I HATE LIFE!' – because he was playing all the time.

If the Jinwoos went out for dinner, Song would play his screen games all through the meal. He wore headphones so he couldn't be distracted by boring things, such as his mum and dad. Mum would spoon food into his mouth and Dad would feed him energy drinks through a straw.

'That's our clever boy,' they said proudly. And they went on spoon-feeding him while he focussed on his games, week after week, month after month, year after year.

When he was five, Song had to go to school. On the first day he went off wearing a baseball cap with a TV screen hanging down from the peak so that he could play on the walk to the playground.

Song wasn't playing a handheld game, though.

He was playing a console, carried in a satchel on his back.

How did he keep it plugged in? you might be wondering. Well, his dad had given him one of those unwinding extra-long extension leads that keeps electrical things running outside. The extension lead played out behind him as he walked, but it caused all sorts of trouble. An old man tripped over it. A cyclist rode into it and went flying over her handlebars.

But the trouble really
started when Song refused to take off his
gaming hat in the classroom.

'I'M PLAYING,' he snarled. 'BACK OFF!' When the
teacher tried to remove it, he bit her on the hand and ran
off, and the power cord got tangled round chair legs and
table legs and children's legs, until everyone and everything
in the classroom were snarled up together.

Song was expelled the same day.

So, his parents decided he could stay at home and learn
by playing educational games instead.

Song found this very dull. Already he was fed up
because he was only able to play with one console at a time.

'Gimme a handheld device too!' Song hollered.

'But you need to learn your lessons, my sweet,' said Mrs
Jinwoo.

'I CAN PLAY WHILE I LEARN, STUPID!' Song roared.

His proud mum rushed to obey. Sure enough, Song
showed her that he could scrape by on his learning game
while still playing first-person shooters on a tablet.

'He's a genius,' Dad declared. 'We should encourage his talents.'

'Yes, you should!' Song shouted. 'Gimme more TVs! More consoles! More handhelds. MORE, MORE, *MORE!*'

Soon, Song's bedroom boasted seventeen screens on one wall, each hooked up to a different device, from the latest experimental consoles to the most clunky, chunky retro games systems you can imagine. Song would spend the day flitting from one to another like a hummingbird (an overweight, very large hummingbird). He played and played until his fingers grew blistered, twisted and totally mangled from constantly clutching controllers.

At that point, you'd think his parents might've stepped in and sorted him out.

Not a bit of it!

While his hands healed, they encouraged Song to play with his feet and toes instead.

And that's exactly what he did. He was soon playing two games at once without lifting a finger. Indeed, he *couldn't* lift a finger, because his mum had wired them up to a special digital-exercise machine she'd designed using motors and rubber bands to help heal his hands and reach new peaks of fingery physical fitness.

It was around then that something rather curious occurred.

One morning, Song woke with a frown. A frown deep enough to tear his eyes away from the screen on the ceiling above his head and the game he'd paused a few hours before. He was frowning because his mum's machine had stopped working. The rubber bands on his hands had caught on something.

When he looked at his left hand, Song couldn't believe what he saw.

The rubber bands had caught on a SECOND THUMB, growing between his first thumb and his index finger.

He gasped and then turned to his right hand – to find a SECOND INDEX FINGER was growing beside the first.

Slowly, Song started to smile.

'It's a dream come true!' he cried, starting to play. Song soon found that his dinky mini-thumb and forefinger were perfect for getting an extra grip on his controller buttons without doubling up. 'I'm going to BOSS these games like never before.'

'MUM! DAD!' he boomed. 'COME HERE, NOW!'

His parents came, and saw, and fell to their knees.

'It's a miracle!' Mum mewed. 'I will remake my machine at once so that it keeps your new digits super-supple too!'

'Yes, do that,' Song snapped. He had no manners, for none of his games taught such things.

'Keep playing, son,' Dad urged. 'You're going to be the greatest gamer in the world.'

'I ALREADY AM!' Song shouted gleefully. 'Keep up, old man! Except you can't, can you? *No one* can keep up with me. I AM THE GREATEST!'

Yes. Young Song truly was an unpleasant toad.

Incredible as it sounds, Song increased his time spent playing. He had screens mounted in the toilet so he could continue games while he did his business, and a sponge on a stick stuck to the ground allowed him to wipe his butt without taking his fingers and thumbs away from his precious controllers. His father put his meals into a blender so he could slurp them up through a straw. Song literally never did anything but play, play, play – on his handhelds, his consoles, his iPod, his iPad, his tablet, his PC, his laptop, his phone, his dad's phone, his mum's phone . . .

And the more he played, the more he went on mutating.

Perhaps it was a mysterious effect of Mum's motorised rubber bands on his hands . . . or perhaps Song absorbed more radiation than most from the many machines he played with all day every day . . . or perhaps it was something in the wireless wavelengths wobbling from his machines 24/7?

Perhaps it might even have been a wicked witchy *curse*? Such things have been known to happen . . .

Whatever it was, Song's eyes slowly turned from ovals to squares, reflecting the many screens he stared at. He grew a whole handful of extra thumbs and fingers, the better to manipulate his multiple controllers. His toes grew longer, more like fingers, and his big toes turned into chunky thumbs. They were a bit clumsy, but that was OK because soon Song grew more of them, tiny toe-fingers and toe-thumbs that were perfect for working little keys on smaller devices.

By the age of twelve, Song was close to achieving his ultimate ambition: to play *all* of his games devices at the same time.

'That's impossible,' I hear you cry, 'even for a mutant genius!'

Incredibly, though, it was true.

I don't know how he did it, but Song really could do several things at once. None of them were useful things, of course, or remotely helpful to anyone else on earth. But then, Song didn't care about anyone else on earth. He only cared about himself and his screen-time.

But what of his parents who had allowed Song to turn into such a technological toad? Well, they couldn't have been happier. They bragged and boasted wherever they went to anyone who would listen:

'Have you seen our son? He's the child of the future!'

'He's got twenty-seven fingers!'

'His eyes are like two perfect screens!'

'He is the next stage in human evolution!'

On and on they went, *burble, burble, burble*. And I'm not sure who exactly was listening closely, nor whom *they* told in turn but, in the end . . .

It was to bring woe to the Jinwoos.

One Thursday night, while Song was playing thirteen games at once in his bedroom, there was an accident. A retro console stored in the garage somehow managed to overheat and – **BOOM!** – it blew up the whole house with a mighty blast. Song was thrown from his bedroom window and wound up dangling from a tree, still playing. He only noticed something was wrong when the power supply completely died and the consoles switched off.

'WHAT IS THE MEANING OF THIS?' he raged, waving his odd little fists.

'Excuse me, Master Jinwoo,' came a smooth voice from below. It was a man in a dark suit with a bright smile. 'I'm so sorry to hear that your house has been blown up by a faulty retro video games console that must have somehow overheated all by itself and with no involvement from anyone else. Such a shame. And yet, these things happen, don't they?'

'I DON'T CARE, JUST SWITCH ON THE POWER, SO I CAN KEEP PLAYING!' Song bellowed.

'I'm also so sorry to have to tell you that your parents have absent-mindedly left the country on a flight to an unknown destination which they must have boarded by accident,' the Man in the Dark Suit went on. 'We don't know when they're coming back, so in the meantime, we are going to look after you.'

'Look after me?' Song sniffed. 'I am the future of Planet Earth! You should *worship* me!'

'Why, yes,' said the Man in the Dark Suit politely. 'That's why we want to take you to a special place where we can . . . er, worship you all day. Worship you for ever.'

'I should hope so too,' said Song, his fingers and thumbs twitching uncontrollably after two minutes without a working screen. 'Get on with it, then.'

'If you insist,' said the Man in the Dark Suit.

That dark, mysterious night, Song Jinwoo disappeared from the world of ordinary folk like you and me (well, you, at least). Because some people the Man in the Dark Suit knew – people who wore suits even darker than his own – believed that Song truly *was* the future of Planet Earth and they wanted to learn what he could do, and what he might go on to do, and what had made him the way that he was.

The Men in Dark Suits built a new home for Song Jinwoo – a big metal cage full of cameras and measurers

and pokers and prodders, with a shiny glass window at the front that looked almost like an enormous screen. Through that screen the Men in Dark Suits could control Song – steer him this way and that, power him up with food, send him to sleep to boost his health . . .

It was almost as if Song were suddenly on the *other* side of the screen, being controlled by unseen players; almost as if *he* were the main character of the game. Not that Song cared! He was too busy playing his various consoles to notice where he was, and he was too stupid to really care.

Don't feel sorry for the foolish little toad. In the end his mum and dad found their way back from wherever they were sent and – eventually – managed to get their son away from the Men in Dark Suits. Mostly because the Men in Dark Suits were thoroughly sick of studying someone so unpleasant and couldn't wait for him to go. On Song's way out, one of the Men in Dark Suits was heard to say, 'If THAT creep is the future of Planet Earth, I'm going to Mars.'

Song shot him a scowling, square-eyed look. 'BRING ME BACK A SCREEN GAME!' he said. And as far as he was concerned, the matter was at –

An End . . .

Or was it . . . **A Beginning?**

All Toads Together!

Well, now! You've met the toadiest toads I've ever come across, and believe me, I've sought out a few in my time. You know what I say – at least, you *ought* to know what I say, since I've said it a great many times – it's never too late to change.

And with that in mind, the other day I invited all the toads in this book to a special party. I thought they could use one. You can't deny that they've all been through a lot, haven't they? Fate taught them each a lesson.

But had they really learned those lessons?

That's what I wondered.

I do like toady tales to have neat endings – don't you?

I was delighted when they all replied to say they would attend my little get-together. Almost as if the invitation was slightly charmed and they had no choice in the matter . . .

And when they did arrive, didn't they get along famously!

Didn't they?

Er, no, they didn't.

They were nasty to each other.

When grown-ups go to parties, they tend to bring a bottle of something nice as a gift for the host, to help jolly things along. Well, Anya Gopopov didn't bring a bottle, she brought an enormous crate of fizzy pop and refused to share it with anybody. She stood in the kitchen burping and guzzling and burping some more.

Anya Gopopov

Jeremiah Bratson

Jeremiah Bratson was not impressed – after being brought back to earth by the aliens, he'd bought his own fizzy drink company, and now every tap in his mansion house runs hot and cold cola. He was showing off about that and also about the ten amazing one-off consoles he owned.

Poor Song Jinwoo was desperate to play them all at once. Well, I say desperate, but he didn't actually look up from the seven screen games he was already playing.

Song Jinwoo

Jacques LaConk

He was probably *more* desperate to ignore Jacques LaConk, who kept asking him to use his mutant fingers and toes to prise yucky stuff from his bottomless nostrils.

I'm surprised young Jacques didn't go the other way and bung up his nose to keep the whiff of Cherry Oddfellow away – she had lapsed into her old mucky ways, and insisted on taking a mud bath before coming to my house.

Cherry Oddfellow

Misha Petal stood beside Cherry for hours, picking the flowers growing out of her muddy skin and crushing them underfoot, the little tyke.

Misha Petal

Hovering not far away was Gustav Munch, boring everyone with the details of how he'd eaten raw flowers, worms and grubs as a natural cure for Meteorite-Face – a medical condition experienced only by nasty boys who get struck by lumps of rock from beyond the stars.

Gustav Munch

He had to shout his silly lies, because Horace and Verdigris Rattlechain were making a racket, screaming and yelling at each other and anyone else who came near, drowning out the delightful

Horace & Verdigris
Rattlechain

chamber-pot music I'd arranged in the front room.

Marco & Rosa Broccoli

As if that wasn't bad enough, Marco and Rosa Broccoli were moaning and groaning about the party food being so healthy (they should've thought themselves lucky – I would've served carrot *sick*, not carrot sticks, if the cat hadn't licked it up before kick-off).

While they bored everyone to death, Hermione Sludge pushed in and stuffed the entire buffet down her young-again throat, saying she'd barely eaten a thing back in Victorian times – and while my party seemed dreadful to her it was, at least, better than SCHOOL.

Dear me, what a dreary party. But it's never too late to change things . . .

So that's exactly what I did.

I changed things.

I changed those little toads into . . .